THE DESERT HAWK

HARRY SINCLAIR DRAGO

SAGEBRUSH
Large Print Westerns

First published in the United States by
The Macaulay Company

First Isis Edition
published 2017
by arrangement with
Golden West Literary Agency

A catalogue record for this book is available
from the British Library.

ISBN 978–1–78541–230–1 (pb)

Published by
F. A. Thorpe (Publishing)
Anstey, Leicestershire

Set by Words & Graphics Ltd.
Anstey, Leicestershire
Printed and bound in Great Britain by
T. J. International Ltd., Padstow, Cornwall

This book is printed on acid-free paper

THE DESERT HAWK

When Aaron Thane's business begins to fail, he
purchases a small ranch in northern Nevada. His
da   rn a
pr   ttle
see   rop
an   But
tro   the
La   ern
Hu   d is
kn   the
sh   uld
rer   : an
ea   her
ou   d of
he   and
sh   . .

This book must be returned by the date specified at the time of issue as
the DATE DUE FOR RETURN.
The loan may be extended (personally, by post, telephone or online) for
a further period if the book is not required by another reader, by quoting
the above number / author / title.

Enquiries: 01709 336774

www.rotherham.gov.uk/libraries

Prologue

Spring came early to the desert country that year. Just before dawn one morning a chinook set in and blew for two days. The snow went off as as if by magic. Little rivulets overran their banks and the usually docile creeks became raging torrents.

The cattle moved up and spread out over the hills. Funny little brockle-faced calves tagged after their mothers, nosing about the snow patches in the arroyos and hunting for the tender green shoots of grass that seemed to have appeared overnight.

While their mammies were foraging the family meal the little fellows often wandered off. If by chance they lost sight of their mothers, they bawled as impatiently as children until they were found, and like children they were awkward, helpless and often obstinate.

On the alkali flats great pools of water formed. Despite the watchful eyes of the old cows the little fellows would attempt to drink the water, often with fatal results. When patience gave out, their mothers would charge them, bellowing angrily, and haze them into the higher hills.

Men began to appear on the range. Outfits which for the winter months had been trimmed down to a foreman, horse wrangler and cook, took on new hands rapidly. The spring round-up would follow almost immediately. Cattle that had roamed all winter long, often drifting for miles, had to be put back on their own range. The country would be gone over with a fine comb. Creek bottoms, cañons, hills — all had to be whipped out thoroughly. After the herd was assembled, the cutting-out process would begin. It would last a day or two. All of the big brands would be represented, for it was the only way of learning how one's stock had wintered.

There were always losses. Even the XL and the Lazy K, the two biggest brands north of the Humboldt, who owned their own range and maintained winter line-camps, always found their tally-books "short." It was part of the game; founded on the proposition that it was cheaper to gamble with weather, rustlers and predatory animals — and lose, than to undertake the enormous expense of proper safeguards.

The winter just past had been mild, so the cattle outfits, big and small, in all that vast square of territory from the Little Humboldt north to the Oregon–Idaho line and west from the Tuscaroras to the Pine Forest Range, faced the spring round-up with less concern than usual.

There was another matter, however, which caused them the gravest concern, and it was a matter of long standing and growing importance. They regarded it as a menace now where once it had been only a threat. It could be summed up in one word ... sheep! The eternal conflict in a semi-arid grazing country.

Fifty years and more had passed since Angel Irosabal and the first Basques had come to the Humboldt country with their flocks. Then, as now, the feud had existed. Word had been passed down the river that sheepmen must stay out. But the Basques clung on and year by year had drawn reinforcements from distant Spain.

They were a thrifty people, immune to hardship and loneliness. They had prospered in the valley of the Humboldt. They asked only to be left alone — a preposterous thing on the face of it. Not because they were Basques and often likened to Mexicans, but because they were herders. Nowhere in the history of man is it written that sheepherders and cattlemen have used the same range in peace. For while cattle may graze forever, sheep in time destroy it.

Looking back over the fifty or more years that had intervened since the first Basque *caserio* had been built in the fertile bottom land of Martins Creek, just above where it flows into the Little Humboldt, there was no escaping the fact that it was the cattlemen who had given way — never the Basque, and this despite the fact that it was the cattle interests that had organized and always proclaimed the deadline beyond which sheep must not graze.

There had been strife — incessant strife, but always the cattlemen had retired. Always they had refused to accept the Basque as a worthy foe. They invented a name of contempt for him; called him a "bosko" (a corruption of the word Basque pronounced with the *que* sounded almost as a second syllable). They ostracized him, turned the law on him whenever possible, and, without question, often cheated him.

It was their way of driving him out. They did not know that through the centuries, princes and generals, without number, had failed to dislodge the Basque from his native valleys and *parameras* in the distant Pyrenees; that neither war nor conquest nor tottering throne had ever materially affected him in his possession of the soil of his fathers.

Had they known, they might have realized their danger in time. In pioneer days, their fathers had said, "No sheep north of the Humboldt!"

If you will look at the map you will see that the battle-line had moved north half the length of the county in the years that had intervened. Paradise Valley, just south of the Santa Rosas, had become largely a Basque town. There were Basque ranchos on Martins Creek and all the other creeks flowing south to the Little Humboldt. Sheep were everywhere.

The Santa Rosa Range runs north and south. To the east of it, above the North Fork, the Basques had never really got a foothold. Stopped there, they had turned back and followed the creeks north through the foothills and also circled around to the west of the range and moved north.

A natural barrier faced them now. Emigrant Creek ran east and west. It was a wild, tangled country, the creek flowing through a deep cañon, its walls sheer and almost impassable. The creek headed among the high

4

peaks of the Santa Rosas, as did practically all of the fifty or more creeks that eventually found their way to the Little Humboldt, the Quinn or the Humboldt proper. Save for the deep cañons and gorges through which the creeks found their way, the mountains rose in a solid granite wall, as impregnable a fortress as any cattleman could have desired.

North from Hinkey Summit, the Santa Rosas unrolled into high plateaus and great swelling upland meadows. From the Summit one could look down on the Basque country spread out below. There, for years, indeed, cattlemen had stood and shook their collective fist at the traditional foe. The only road to the top was a circuitous one, winding through deep defiles and clinging crazily to the narrow shoulders of great mountains.

A handful of men might have held that road against an army. But the battle was never to be fought there, for a benign government, its motives so mysterious as to defy solution, reduced most of that natural barrier, which had seemed so impregnable, and which well might have preserved the existing status quo forever, to invisible lines. It was done with the pen that signed the bill creating the Santa Rosa table-lands and watershed a National Forest!

Thousands of acres of grazing land were included within its boundaries — range that cattlemen had used either on lease or successfully poached on since the days of the free range. It was incredible. Forest Reserve? Why the country was almost treeless! There were willows along the creek beds, and some poplar and dwarf cedar, perhaps even a sprinkling of piñon and birch. But forest? It was to laugh!

Yet no cattleman could summon even a grin to his lips in appreciation of the jest. It was a trick. To a man they believed the Basques were at the bottom of it. The old hatred flamed anew. Some said they would not move out. But they did, and when they moved out, the rangers moved in.

The big brands appealed to the law, but the law could do nothing for them: the leaseholds would not be renewed. Grazing permits allowing cattle to run in the Reserve at so much per head, could be applied for, however, and they would be issued in the order received. The Government reserved the right to decide how much stock the Reserve could support without injury to it.

The cattlemen breathed a sigh of relief, but before they could take a second breath, they learned that cattlemen and herder were to be treated alike; if a Basque applied for a permit, his request would be honored in turn.

In vain did they protest that cattle would not graze on the same land with sheep. Quite as idle was their contention that sheep would destroy as much grass as they ate, grazing it to the roots and grinding what remained to powder beneath their sharp hoofs. The Department was sorry, but the regulations in effect in other Forest Reserves and National Parks must govern here.

The Basque *genté* was quite as stunned as the cattle outfits. They were innocent of any conniving in the matter, it seems needless to add. Indeed they could not believe this good fortune was really theirs, so used had they become to taking the leavings. Experience had taught them never to expect anything for nothing. Now suddenly they were asked to believe in a miracle. No wonder they were suspicious.

For years they had dreamed of fattening their sheep in the Santa Rosas. In dry years, when their range failed completely, their sheep had died in hundreds, while cattle grew fat in the creek bottoms and high hills to the north. Now all that was to be changed. Drouth and dry years were to lose their terror. It meant unheard prosperity and happiness.

Even old Angel Irosabal, the head of his elan and headman of all his people, a wise, shrewd and thrifty leader, shook his head. It was too good to be true. There must be a catch somewhere.

With characteristic caution, he advised his people to wait. Lambing-time was at hand with its hard work and endless worries. Let it engage the attention of all. When it was over there would be time to discuss this new problem.

It was sound advice. Almost to a man they accepted it, content to be guided by the patriarch who had led them to this new land and helped them to prosper.

But if the Basque *genté* waited, the cattlemen did not. No better opportunity for discussing their grievances and methods of resistance could have been devised than was afforded by the spring round-up. Every brand was represented, even some that had no stock on the range. This new order of things affected all, and in that very tender spot known as the pocketbook.

They were no longer standing with their backs to the wall. There was some degree of safety in even such a precarious position as that. They were caught between two fires, now. This was the last stand, and they knew it. The old Cattleman's Association was a defunct organization utterly unable to cope with such a situation as this.

They swore vengeance and once more had recourse to threats.

"No sheep north of Emigrant Creek or in the Reserve," was the warning that rumbled down into the Basque country. The Basque smiled; he had been warned before. The cattle outfits had a habit of arrogating certain rights to themselves. But how could they enforce their will?

Old Angel did not smile when the warning was repeated to him. The plight of the cowmen was too desperate to hold any hope that the coming struggle would resolve itself into a mere battle of threats and warnings. For fifty years, more or less, cowboy and herder had carried on their feud, and the issue had never been decided. It seemed now that the end might well be in sight. He knew, deny it though he often did, that either cattle or sheep must go; both could not stay. Once let the flocks on the Reserve, and the big herds soon would be a thing of the past.

But that would not be easily accomplished. There would be armed resistance, bloodshed, reprisals — and every form of intimidation resorted to that desperate

8

men could devise. Both sides must inevitably run afoul of the law. Nevada had changed to that extent.

And yet, for all his gloomy foreboding, he welcomed the struggle that was so surely coming. His people had prospered in the valley of the Humboldt, but they had suffered, too. Hardly an inch had they gained that had not been dearly paid for. Contempt and insult had been the portion meted out to them. But they had never given ground in the face of it, and he knew they would not give ground now.

He called his sons and grandsons to his side, and even as they gathered, a dozen men, who had met secretly at the Lazy K ranch, pushed back their chairs and reached for their hats, with faces just as solemn as his. They realized, even as he, that this was the final showdown, that the winner would take all. If they lost, they must move on — following the grass to some new country, even as the Basques had done in coming to the valley of the Humboldt.

It was a moment calling for desperate measures. If they went down, they would go down fighting. The time for talking and empty warnings was over.

CHAPTER
ONE

A Rift in the Barrier

The day was unusually warm for early May. In the deep ravines patches of snow still lingered, although the hillsides were already beginning to lose their mantle of green. The wind that rustled the leaves of the tall poplars in the Lazy K ranch-yard was as invigorating as wine. The air was bracing too, and so clear that the little bunches of cattle grazing contentedly on the steep slopes of Mount Misery were plainly discernible. Not a cloud flecked the deep blue of the heavens, but at a great height an enormous hawk sailed lazily against the wind, its wings spread out flat as boards.

The uncurtained windows of the ranch-house stood open, and flies droned noisily in the white-washed rooms. From the rear of the house came the voice of Chang, the Chinese cook, raised in song, his version of a popular American ragtime tune of the day. The effect was weird enough to startle the most devout disciple of syncopation.

Save for Chang's singing, the Lazy K seemed to slumber in the noontime majesty of the spring day. Suddenly, however, a door banged noisily and a man stuck out his head.

"You goin' to keep up that caterwaulin' all day?" he scolded angrily. "Cut it out!" There was no answer from the kitchen, but the singing stopped abruptly.

The tall man who had come to the door scanned the valley which led up to Lazy K. He was about to turn indoors when he caught himself and raised his hand to shade his eyes. A tiny little dust-cloud had caught his attention. He watched it until certain that it was moving toward the Lazy K.

"That'll be Bridger, now," he mused aloud. He pulled out his watch and glanced at it impatiently. "Certainly took his time!" he muttered, and turned back to the room that served him as an office.

His impatience did not subside as he waited, but in the five years he had been in Humboldt County Jim Cantrell had won the reputation of being perpetually impatient, short of temper and a bad man to cross.

Under him the Lazy K had made money. He was only a part owner of the brand, but his partner never interfered with his management of the property, although Del Ryan, Humboldt County's political boss, was the power behind the throne.

Cantrell was no longer young, but there was grace in his movements and more than a hint of strength in his wiry, well-knit frame. He was over six feet tall, and perhaps it was his great height that gave him the appearance of being overly thin. What there was of him was all steel and whipcord. The men who worked for him hated him, as a rule, but because he was a hard-riding, untirable whirlwind in the saddle, never asking of a man what he couldn't and wouldn't do himself, he won the allegiance of some.

He was rather handsome in a cold, saturnine way, his eyes black and piercing and features well chiseled. His mouth was cruel and forbidding, however, and the wisp of black mustache which fringed it did not soften it.

No one looking for a soft berth ever thought of applying to Cantrell for a job. When he gave an order it had to be obeyed instantly, or someone got his "time." Fortunately few orders were necessary. Hank Rude, Uncle Henry to the Lazy K crowd, saw to that. He was the buffer that kept peace in the family.

Fully half an hour must pass before the approaching rider could arrive. Cantrell threw his legs upon his littered desk and leaned back in his chair until he was stretched out almost horizontally. With a cigar in his mouth and his hat pulled down over his eyes, he settled himself to wait. The flies annoyed him and he cursed and slapped at them ineffectually.

The room was almost bare. A map of the newly created Santa Rosa National Forest flamed on the wall, its white margin finger-marked and already covered with penciled notations. The floor was without rugs and evidently had not been swept in some time. Two rifles reposed in a corner behind the desk. In the opposite corner of the room stood a small safe. Someone had dumped an old saddle on top of it, and judging by the dust which covered it, it had been there a long while. These objects, the desk, two chairs and a dilapitated calendar, the advertising gift of a Winnemucca hardware dealer, completed the furnishings of the room.

Its windows did not command a view of the road which led up from the valley. When half an hour had passed and the visitor had not arrived, Cantrell flung his feet to the floor and tramped to the door.

"It's him, all right," he exclaimed. "You'd think he was goin' to a funeral the way he pokes along."

A few minutes later the horseman rode into the yard, and on seeing Cantrell, waved a pudgy hand at him. "Getting dusty already," he called. His clothes were white with it.

He was a short, stocky man, his face round as a ball. Save for his pink cheeks he was as colorless as the dust that he brushed from his shoulders and wide Stetson. The desert suns of many years had bleached his squinting eyes and hair. His clothes were faded, too. And yet, there was an air of importance about him that transcended his shabby appearance.

"I was goin' to town to-day," Cantrell exclaimed. "Thought you'd be here earlier than this."

"I would 'a' been here sooner if I hadn't heard something and stopped to investigate it. We got something more important to talk about now than whether you want to buy some breeders or not."

Cantrell shot him a questioning glance.

"What do you mean?" he demanded.

Bridger looked around as if to make sure that they were alone. Chang had just rung the dinner-bell. Four Lazy K men were approaching from the direction of the corrals.

"Let's go inside," said he. "We can talk this thing over privately."

It was impossible to escape the difference between the two men as they walked side by side to the house. Chris Bridger owned the biggest cattle outfit in northern Humboldt County. His brand, the Diamond Dot, was known all over the state. He was rich, for his time. He had been born on the Humboldt. His father before him had run cattle. He was the product of a school of hard knocks; shrewd, taciturn, a good trader, one who never let his honesty stand in the way of his own best interests, as his present affluence so eloquently testified. In his day, the universal intention had been to get it while the getting was good. Times had changed, but old Chris had not changed with them.

He was slow to anger, a cool thinker, as a rule, whose logic was always better than his eloquence. Cantrell, on the other hand, was a firebrand, whose vehemence often outweighed his judgment. And yet, because he was aggressive and a Basque hater as well as baiter, men like Bridger had come to regard him as their leader.

"Well, what is it?" Cantrell demanded as soon as they entered his office.

Old Chris was not to be hurried.

"Did you hear that Jenkins had sold his place?" he asked when he had dashed off the drink that Cantrell offered.

"I heard he was aimin' to sell," Big Jim replied.

"Well, he closed the deal last week."

14

"That's all right, ain't it?"

"All right, nothing!" Old Chris exclaimed. "Jenkins always wanted me to buy him out. I didn't want his place. Water enough on it, but you can't git to it. All that Emigrant Creek cañon belonged to him. As for range, what did he have? I knew he would never sell out to a Basque without givin' me first chance. So I never worried any about the place. I wish to God I'd bought it now!"

"Why, I thought he was dickering with that tenderfoot from back East. What's his name — Thane?"

"That's him, a dodderin' old fool that ain't got no business in this yere country. You know what we said, Cantrell, about no sheep comin' north of the creek? Well, they're a-comin', and ain't no Basque bringin' 'em, either. Thane's hired his herders already, he's aimin' to run sheep!"

Cantrell's face went white with rage.

"What, a white man throwin' in with the boskos?" he cried. "Goin' to run sheep, huh! Oh, no he ain't! No man, greaser or white, is comin' north of the creek with sheep!" and he banged his desk violently with his clenched fist. "He'll change his mind or we'll change it for him."

"'Tain't him we got to fight, it's his daughter."

"What! he's got a woman with him?"

"Yep, and she's the boss, if I know anythin'. She's a swell looker, Jim."

"Humph!" was all the answer Cantrell made.

"I'm afraid she's goin' to complicate matters considerable." Bridger ran on. "Some of our crowd won't stand for handin' out to her the gravel we're aimin' to give the Basque *genté*."

"You leave her to me," Cantrell said menacingly; "I know how to handle women. Did you threaten her?"

"Well," old Chris smiled, "I gave her a pretty strong hint there'd be trouble if her pa stuck to his plans."

"What'd she say?"

"Said her pa was an honest, God-fearin' man; that all they wanted was their rights."

"And I suppose she quoted the law to you? Well, we'll grab a bite to eat and ride over there this afternoon. I reckon we got rights, too, and we ain't goin' to be talked out of 'em by any one, man or woman."

"You're right, there, Jim, but the trouble that's comin' is goin' to be bad. There's been killin's before, and I reckon it'll git to that this time. It ain't goin' to be no place for a woman; we got to git her out."

"You leave that to me, I tell you! She'll go."

"I don't know, Jim. I got the idea she's goin' to be mighty hard to skeer!"

Half an hour later they were in the saddle and riding east.

As they rode away, two of Cantrell's men came to the door of the dining-room and stared after them.

"Going east, Lin, just as you figgered," said the older of the two, a freckle-faced, red-haired man whose legs were noticeably bowed.

The man referred to as Lin, he was not over twenty-five, nodded grimly. He was a good-looking boy, with black curly hair, level, wide-set gray eyes that just now were as cold as ice.

"Goin' to throw the fear of God into those folks, I suppose," he drawled. "There's some things I draw the line at, Flash. This is one of them; I don't make war on women, sheep or no sheep."

"And sheep's at the bottom of this. I guessed as much as soon as I saw Bridger ride in," Flash McCarroll muttered as Lin and he walked toward the corrals where they were breaking horses. "I could 'a' told Cantrell the news yesterday. Wait till you see this gal, you old heartbreaker!" and he gave Lin a resounding slap on the back.

"What'd you say she was called?"

"Frazier Thane!"

"Sounds like a boy's name."

"Well, she is kind-a like a boy," Flash declared. "When she looks at you her eyes go right through you."

"Certainly had a fatal effect on you," Lin answered dryly. "Couldn't even tell her the way home, eh?"

"I was too plumb scared, I told you! It was about two minutes before I could talk!" the red-haired man exploded. "But she's just a baby, Lin; don't know nuthin' about this country. I always been a sheep hater, but if she can stand for 'em, I reckon I can."

Lin Kincaid's lips straightened. There was something reckless and hot-tempered about the set of his mouth. "I'm afraid she and her father are up against a stacked deck," he murmured. "They shouldn't ever have come in here."

"I agree with you, Lin. But they're here."

"And they ought to get a square shake."

"But they won't, unless someone like you and me sorta looks out for 'em. Come on! if we git done in time we'll just drift over that-a-way toward evenin', just accidental-like, an' see how the land lies."

"I was wonderin' why you shaved this mornin'," Lin grinned.

"Shaved?" Flash snorted. "Why, daggone it, I know a lady when I see one," and he climbed into the corral bawling at the top of his voice:

"Old Ben Bolt was a blamed good boss.
But he'd go to see the girls on a sore-backed
    hoss.
It's cloudy in the west, a lookin' like rain.
And my damned old slicker's in the wagon
    again!"

But of the "Chisholm Trail" there were forty verses, and Flash knew them all, and in addition, forty more of his own making.

CHAPTER
TWO

Frazier Thane

The old Jenkins place, which Aaron Thane had purchased, was a small ranch as ranches go in northern Nevada. Ad Jenkins had owned it for fifteen years. In that time he had made few improvements.

Some people said Ad was unfortunate; others that he was just lazy. However that may be, he certainly never took more than a frugal living off his ranch. But he was a bachelor, so no one was ever unduly concerned over his prosperity or lack of it.

Ad had accepted his lot philosophically. His favorite adage was ever that "one man's gain is another man's loss" — a thought that he must have expressed to himself as he pocketed Aaron Thane's dollars, for now that he had finally sold out, it was popularly supposed that he had unloaded at a good price — which was true.

It is rather hard to understand the urge that drives men well along in life, over sixty in Aaron Thane's case, to give up the comparative prosperity of small businesses, won at the cost of the best efforts of their robust years, to try their fortunes in a new land and in a calling about which they know absolutely nothing at all, foregoing old friendships and all the comfortable and stable associations of a lifetime.

Back in Great Barrington, Massachusetts, Aaron Thane had once been regarded as a substantial citizen. The hardware business, which his father had bequeathed him, seemed to prosper in his hands.

He was a proud man, prone at times to remind you that the Thanes had been among the original settlers of the Commonwealth, and at the slightest provocation he could be depended on to launch into the heartiest defense of every New England tradition, a geographical and cultural section of the United States which he still believed represented its best political and business thought.

He was deeply religious, rockbound in his convictions and altogether the sort of man who might have been expected to live and die in the peaceful valleys of his fathers. And yet, when as a young man he had looked about him for a wife, he had journeyed to Pennsylvania for his mate, marrying one of the Pennsylvania Fraziers.

A discerning mind might have seen in that some evidence of the adventurous spirit and flair for the unknown which, later in life, were to tear him away from Great Barrington and make him risk his all on a dream that was not so different from that which had excited the imagination of every pioneer.

As the years passed, there must have been those in Great Barrington who knew that all was not well with Aaron Thane's business. The town had changed; New England had changed. New competitors with modern ideas of business had come to Great Barrington. Business had dwindled; expenses had increased.

It was a rather old story, and yet Aaron Thane believed his changed fortune was due solely to the mail-order houses. The thought became an obsession with him, and so bitter did he grow in his hatred for all things connected with the mail-order business that if by chance he learned one of his customers had purchased aught of them he would lay in wait like some avenging fury and pounce upon the unlucky individual at the first opportunity, soundly beating him and accusing him not only of disloyalty to himself but to the town at large.

The upshot of this was that he usually lost the customer forever. The accumulative result of such tactics hurried the end. But then, Aaron Thane would have failed anyhow. He was too pink and white, too much of the old school to ever hope to cope with the new.

And yet, possibly because she was the most concerned, not a hint of the impending disaster reached the ears of Frazier Thane, old Aaron's motherless daughter, although she could not esape the fact that her father had become less communicative than usual.

She was a proud and beautiful girl of nineteen at the time, in her third year at Holyoke, and looking forward, as most girls of her years do, to those pleasant days immediately following college. Therefore it was to her utter bewilderment that old Aaron informed her, when she returned home for the Christmas vacation that year, that he had sold his business and was going west.

The homestead was on the market. When it was disposed of, she was to follow him.

It was no longer possible for him to conceal from her the sorry state his business had been in for the past few years. Her chagrin and disappointment were keen, but she was loyal and courageous enough not to offer any word of censure, although she could not view without misgiving his determination to try his lot in the west. Intuition warned her that he was a lamb among wolves.

Having once been a "somebody" in Great Barrington, it was true that she did not relish the thought of staying there to teach school or the like. And yet, Nevada seemed so far away and the business of ranching so foreign to the retailing of hardware that she has sorely tried to muster a smile and an encouraging word with which to bid old Aaron Godspeed.

Once free of the fetters that had bound him so long, Aaron Thane became a boy again, thrilling to his own adventure, and although he did not travel in a covered wagon or with a trusty rifle across his knees, he became an intrepid pioneer to himself, smiling benignantly on this new land to which he had come, ready to give it the benefit of his sage wisdom and sober advice as well as the more practical encouragement of his New England dollars.

He was a man made to order for Ad Jenkins. But to his dying day Ad never ceased wondering how much more he might have got out of Aaron if he had only had the nerve to ask it.

Frazier had followed her father almost immediately. Since coming to Nevada she had had no occasion to change her mind about the folly of the step her father had taken. She had learned what a multitude of sins the word "ranch" can cover.

The house to which her father brought her was not much more than a cabin. Ad Jenkins had never been noted for cleanliness. She had expected to put up with inconveniences, but in her first siege of homesickness she found Nevada crude, bleak and inexorable; distances interminable and neighbors nonexistent; ranching but another name for the quickest and shortest route to poverty.

There was compensation in part for those mighty elms that march up and down the streets of Great Barrington, and which she missed so sorely. When the afternoon sun was splashing the rimrocks of Mount Misery with orange and vermilion, and the clean mountain wind brought to her nostrils the pungent fragrance of the young sage, she almost forgot to be lonely. But when night came and the coyotes barked in the hills, cold shivers ran down her spine, and she wondered if she should ever feel at home in Nevada.

The stern necessity of making the ranch pay became her immediate concern. Since one runs either sheep or cattle that decision had to be made immediately. The way to a profit with cattle is long, arduous and often uncertain. With sheep there is the lure of a double crop, quick profits and smaller investment. So quite naturally the Thanes elected to go in for sheep, since Ad Jenkins had been careful not to mention how matters stood, even though old Chris was so sure that Ad would never have sold out to a Basque.

Bridger's visit that morning had brought her first intimation of trouble, although her father had learned enough in Paradise to give him some inkling of what they faced. But it was too late to back out now, even if such a thought had occurred to him. He chose to say nothing to Frazier. It had not been difficult for him to hire a herder. Indeed he had found the Basques a kind, hospitable people, quite willing to do business with him, and accompanied by Bonafacio, the Basque boy whom he had hired, he left for the valley that morning to bring home the first of his flock.

Frazier was still pondering over what she had taken from Bridger's brief visit when she looked up to see two horsemen approaching. She recognized Bridger at once. A few minutes later Chris and Cantrell rode up to the house.

"Yore pa got home yet?" Chris asked in the tone of a neighbor just dropping in for a minute.

"No, he has not," Frazier replied, her uneasiness not lessening as she studied Cantrell.

Bridger introduced them with a word. "Too bad he ain't got back yet," he went on. "Jim and I rode over to have a little talk with him."

"Reckon he'll be back soon," Cantrell smiled. His appraising glance was one of approval. She was even prettier than Bridger had said, and pretty in a way that was new to Cantrell. He tried to beat down her eyes, but it was his own that fell. "Nice place you got here," he said for want of something to say.

"It will do for the present," Frazier replied.

The sunlight touched her hair and it shone like polished copper. Cantrell's gaze had returned to her eyes. They fascinated him in a way. There was fire and determination in their hazel depths. Instinctively he knew that she would not be bluffed. But Cantrell was aware that a more personal equation than had to do with the business that brought him there was running through his mind.

"Sure looks better than it did when Ad Jenkins had the place," old Chris declared honestly. "Ad w'an't no housekeeper at all. I guess you know."

"I certainly do," Frazier laughed.

Cantrell's pulse quickened as he listened. Her laugh was like singing mountain-water breaking over the bowlders in some crystal clear pool. He wished he had come alone. Big Jim had always prided himself on his affairs with women. He believed himself a connoisseur of feminine beauty; but the girl before him was of a finer vintage than any he had known.

He noted her rounded arms and beautifully turned ankles, her poise and carriage and graceful figure, and was more impressed than ever, with the result that he made himself several promises. One was that this was not his last visit to the Thane ranch. He also began to make certain reservations and revisions concerning his errand of to-day. Bridger was right, you couldn't treat this girl like a Basque. Well, it was up to her to say what sort of treatment she wanted; he'd be reasonable if she would. With him looking out for her, things might not be so bad.

Of course Cantrell was in quite the same position as the boy who wanted to eat his cake and have it too. He stood pat on his boast that no sheep were coming north of the creek; but how he hoped to enforce that edict and at the same time advance his own interests with Frazier Thane is a matter that only Cantrell could have answered.

Frazier was aware of his close scrutiny. Her blood turned cold under it, for the light in Big Jim's eyes was too plain to be misunderstood. But she stood her ground, determined that neither one should carry away the idea that they had only a helpless girl with which to deal.

Bridger waited for Cantrell to broach the subject on their visit, but he seemed in no hurry, and it was Frazier who really forced the issue.

"If you have come to see Father about anything concerning the ranch," said she, "I believe I can answer for him. It's about the sheep, I presume."

Old Chris nodded phlegmatically; what else could there be to discuss?

"That's what we wanted to see yore pa about," said he, and his tone implied that they came with an ultimatum.

"Thought we might get him to change his mind," Cantrell declared. "There ain't likely to be no money in sheep this year, nohow."

His manner was so conciliatory that Bridger shot him a quick, reproving glance. Certainly Big Jim had changed his tune, Chris thought, if this was a sample of what was to come. It was just tactics of this sort that was responsible for the whole damnable mess they were in. Chris was not advocating violence this early, but he believed a spade should be called a spade.

"It's too late now for Father to change his mind," Frazier exclaimed patiently. "His money is invested in the ranch and it must earn a living for us. I assure you our sheep will not trespass on your range."

"It ain't that, Miss Thane, that's worryin' us," Chris declared heatedly. "For fifty years sheepmen have been pushing us back. We ain't goin' no further, I can tell yuh! This country north of the creek is still cattle-country, and that's the way it'll stay."

"But Mr. Jenkins didn't tell us we couldn't run sheep."

"What?"

Chris and Cantrell uttered the exclamation as one man.

"He was one of your friends," Big Jim muttered sarcastically.

"I'll make a note of that in case I ever meet up with him," Bridger replied. Luckily for Ad, he was through with Nevada. "It's too bad he roped you in that-a-way," he continued to Frazier, "but bein' sorry don't help it none. I'm goin' to enlighten you on the way matters stand."

He sat down on the porch without waiting to be invited and motioned to Cantrell to do the same.

"This thing goes way back, and I'm goin' to tell you all of it so as you can see we ain't unreasonable," he began, and without further preamble or introduction recounted the bitter feud that had lasted for half a century. Whenever Frazier seemed unable to understand the point Chris was trying to make, Cantrell threw in an enlightening word.

The story was told from the cowman's viewpoint of course, and colored accordingly. Some of it was so partisan as to make Frazier smile to herself at the man's naïveté. At least it acquainted her with what she and her father faced. She could not comprehend all of the details of the sanguinary feud of Basque and cattleman, but what she did understand convinced her that something was to be said on both sides.

Bridger spoke of the cattlemen's rights — but he was hopelessly vague on the subject of who had invested his side with those much-abused rights. They had been the first on the ground; that was enough. Priority constituted a title in their eyes.

Frazier thought that rather absurd, for even in the days of the feudal barons it had taken might as well as right to enforce and establish conquests less fanciful than any cattleman's claim to the valley of the Humboldt.

Might had been used, and once again it had become a case of the survival of the fittest — not so much of men as of animals. Sheep can find a living almost anywhere; cattle cannot. That was, and would continue to be, the determining factor.

But Frazier failed to see how all this affected her father and her. What had been had been. Certainly they could not be held accountable for the transgressions of others. Under the constituted authority of the state they held a legal title to the ranch, and both state and nation guaranteed them all those other rights of freedom from oppression which, until now, they had taken as a matter of course. What right had these men to say what her father could or could not do on his own property?

"I'm sorry, gentlemen, I may be dense, but I cannot understand why you should be so concerned over what we do on our own ranch," said she.

"You can't?" Bridger shouted, losing his temper rapidly, for he realized that his argument had failed to have the desired effect. "Well, by God, I'll show you!"

"Now they ain't no cause for your flyin' off like that!" Cantrell exclaimed. This, coming from him, left old Chris speechless for a moment.

He gave his companion a withering look but nodded apologetically to Frazier.

"You just overlook that," he went on. "If I git excited it's because I got somethin' to git excited about. If you was jest aimin' to run a small band of sheep here on yore own place, I don't suppose I'd have a call to go rarin' off. But I know you ain't got range enough to keep a band goin'. Yore pa is aimin' to apply for a Reservation permit, same as the boskos. Now that's where it hits me. In a dry year, and this is goin' to be one — they wa'n't much snow the past winter — there ain't grass enough in the Reserve to care for the cattle, let alone any sheep. You talk about makin' a livin'. Am I goin' to sit back and see you take my livin' away from me?

"But the Reserve belongs to all of us; the law says so."

"I wouldn't bank too much on the law," Cantrell muttered.

"Now yore talkin'!" Bridger exclaimed sharply. "We'll make some laws of our own. I reckon a Basque will think twice before he brings his sheep into these hills, permit or no permit."

"I am afraid they've made up their minds to get their rights in the matter," Frazier answered stoutly.

"Well, they'll change their minds, or we'll change them for 'em. I don't want to be hard on you; yo're white folks. But they ain't no sheep goin' on the Reserve no matter who they belong to! You tell yore pa that. There's goin' to be hell to pay here; it ain't no place for a lone woman like you."

Cantrell tried to catch Bridger's eye to warn him to go easy, but old Chris had the bit in his teeth.

"There's ways of persuadin' people that you never heered about back East. I've been through these things before, and I know. When men git excited they ain't no tellin' what they'll do. Don't you wait till it's too late!"

Chris got to his feet and Cantrell did likewise. Frazier's poise had not deserted her. Her fighting ancestors had not been appalled when the odds were against them. The heritage they had bequeathed her became her armor now.

"I may be a lone woman, as you so quaintly put it, Mr. Bridger," she declared proudly, "but you will find I do not frighten easily. I thank you for your interest and advice, but I cannot accept it. I do not know what the Basques intend doing, but I assure you we will not be run out. We have no intention of invading your rights. If you invade ours, we shall fight."

"You may change yore mind," Chris exclaimed tersely as he got into his saddle. "At least you've been warned."

Cantrell rode up close to the porch as Bridger started off. "Maybe I can fix up matters," he murmured under his breath. "I'll drop over to-morrow."

Frazier shook her head. She found him not hard to understand. "I'm afraid you would be only wasting your time, Mr. Cantrell," she replied.

"Don't let that worry you Miss Thane," Big Jim smiled knowingly. "I got time to waste when you're concerned."

CHAPTER
THREE

No Trespassing!

Old Chris glared at Cantrell when the latter caught up with him. He was so angry that the ends of his mustache stood as erect as two little horns.

Cantrell was in no pleasant mood, either.

"What's eatin' you?" he snapped before Bridger could speak.

"I'll tell yuh in a hurry!" Chris thundered. "If that's your idea of gittin' these people out of here, I'm through with you now. Do you think any wishy-washy talk like yours is goin' to make 'em move? Not on yore life!"

"When you get done, I'll talk," Cantrell answered hotly. "Didn't you tell me we couldn't treat her like a bosko? There's more than one way of skinnin' a cat."

"You don't fool me, Cantrell! That gal knocked you for a twister. It's yore own business if you want to play around with her. But that don't mean the bars is goin' to be let down because you're sweet on her. Oh, you needn't talk; I got you right away. I thought you was goin' to cry for her!"

"Don't you ride me too hard, Bridger," Cantrell warned, his face a pasty white. "You talk a lot, but you don't say anythin'. If you want to get through with me, go ahead. For twenty-five years you've been rantin' around just like you're doin' now. And what's it got you? The way you was runnin' things you'd had Basques herdin' sheep on your doorstep by now if I hadn't got busy. I'm the one that's thrown the gaff into 'em, not you! Don't you forget it again. If you'd let me handle that girl I'd got somewhere. I ain't so sure I won't even yet. You leave her to me. She'll be reasonable, or I'll know why!"

"Well, you play square with me, Cantrell," Chris grumbled. "Don't you make her any promises you can't keep."

Cantrell's rage did not subside, but he was shrewd enough to hold his tongue.

Two miles from the Thane place Cottonwood Creek cut across the road. Cantrell's line followed this creek all the way to the Reservation. The opposite bank marked the point farthest north that the Basques had reached. There had been trouble along the creek any number of times. Whether by accident or design the Basque boys had often been caught with their flocks on the wrong side of the creek.

The sheep had always been put off. On one memorable occasion Cantrell had arrived with his rifle and pumped lead until the barrel was so hot he could no longer hold it.

The Basques found ways in which to retaliate, and as a result the creek bottom saw little of the Lazy K cattle, which was gall and wormwood to Cantrell.

To-day, as he and Bridger neared the creek, he cocked his ears suddenly and held up his hand for Chris to rein up. Both men listened together.

"What is it?" Bridger demanded a moment later as they went on.

"Thought I heard sheep baain'."

They quickened their pace. Cantrell was the first to top the little rise that fell away to the creek bottom on the other side.

"By God!" he swore, "there they are! Look at 'em, bunched out over there as though they owned the place!"

He didn't wait for Bridger, but raked his horse with his spurs and dashed down to the creek and crossed it in a shower of flying spray. The day had been an inauspicious one for him. His tilt with Bridger still rankled in his heart. To find this flock of sheep trespassing on his range was the last straw.

He whipped out his six-gun as he rode. His mouth had stretched out into a narrow slit. His black eyes burned in his bloodless face.

The madness of his approach caused the sheep to mill immediately. The barking of the dogs added to the din. An old ram merged from the flock and raced away across Cantrell's range. The next second the flock was streaming after him.

Cantrell shouted and swore. He looked around for Bridger. Chris was just in back of him. "Come on!" Big Jim shouted, "head 'em off!"

He circled around the sheep and began fanning his gun. It was impossible to miss at that distance. Every time he pulled the trigger a sheep went down. The flock had doubled up on itself and now seemed intent only on getting back to the creek.

Cantrell reloaded his gun and kept up the slaughter. The Basque herder, who had been asleep down the creek, now came on the dead run, shouting wildly and waving his arms.

"*Válgame Dios!*" he cried as he saw what had occurred. He recognized Cantrell. "Stop, *Señor*," he shouted, "eet ees mistak' they get across the creek. I shut my eye for two three minutes and theece happen. I get heem back *immediatamente!*"

The boy started across the creek. Cantrell waved him back.

"You stay where you are!" he ordered. "You set foot on my range and you'll get what your sheep got. I'll get 'em off!"

"Oh, no, *Señor!*" the boy pleaded as Cantrell continued to blaze away with his gun. He knew he would have to answer to his elders for this, and that it had occurred through his negligence would not lessen his punishment. His sheep were trespassing, but they could be put off without resorting to merciless slaughter.

Of course they had trespassed many times — there was that to be said in Cantrell's favor. There had been warning after warning.

As a Basque, the boy, Cèsar, hated Cantrell more than he feared him, and had he been armed there might have been a different story to tell. Even unarmed he dared to defy the big cowman. Picking up a bowlder, he leaped halfway across the narrow creek.

The madness of the moment had got into Bridger's veins, too. He was watching the boy closely and sensed his intention.

"Git back thar!" he yelled.

Cèsar did not stop. Cantrell turned to find the boy before him, his arm drawn back to hurl the rock at him.

"You would, eh?" Big Jim mocked. "Well, take that, you damned grease-ball, since you're askin' for it!" and raising his gun, he shot the boy down with as little compunction as he felt in killing his sheep.

Cèsar rolled over on his face and lay still. Then, with the smoking gun still in his hand, Cantrell began to consider the consequences of his deed. Bridger had sobered also.

"Hell will pop now," he murmured. "That boy was an Irosabal — one of old Angel's grandsons!"

"I know it!" Cantrell snapped, desperate all of a sudden. "Let 'em make the most of it! This is only the beginnin'. If they want war, they can have it!"

It was not that he was trying to absolve himself in Bridger's eyes; Cantrell was only driving home the thought that this cruel and wanton blow had been struck in a mutual cause and not from any personal motive.

Bridger understood him perfectly.

"What are you goin' to do with him?" he asked stolidly.

"Leave him right there! They'll be lookin' for him by mornin'. I reckon what they find will tell its own story. Let's go!"

36

Herders had been killed in the past and no great effort had ever been made to bring the guilty parties to justice. So Cantrell was not unduly concerned over what he had done. And yet, as they rode off, he purposely followed the creek for half a mile or more before striking dry land. Even Bridger appreciated the advisability of not leaving a trail that could be easily followed.

The sun was beginning to sink in the west by the time they left Cottonwood Creek. Cantrell turned toward the north and home; Chris continued on west to the Diamond Dot on Quinn River.

They had resolved to say nothing; leaving it to whoever was interested to prove who was the guilty party or parties. Instead of striking back to the road. Cantrell went on over the hills. A mile from the house, he encountered Uncle Henry, the Lazy K foreman. They rode home together. Uncle Henry had routine matters to discuss. He found nothing unusual in Cantrell's manner.

"Been over to see those folks that bought out Jenkins," Big Jim offered. "Struck across the hills on the way home." A statement which, if true, would have made him cross Cottonwood Creek two miles north of the scene of the slaughter.

Old Hank had questions to ask about the newcomers. Cantrell was glad to keep the conversation in that channel.

"This Thane girl seems to have knocked our boys a twister," Uncle Henry chuckled.

Cantrell's brow clouded. "Who?"

"Well, Flash for one. Kincaid and him broke their necks gittin' through this afternoon so as they could go to town. They ain't got no idea of goin' to town!"

"I'm glad you mentioned this, Hank. You find a little more work for them after this. And by the way, with trouble comin', I ain't wantin' my men gittin' thick with this Thane girl. That's an order from now on!"

CHAPTER
FOUR

"You've Got Friends!"

Lin and Flash had been gone some time when Cantrell got in. Of course they had no intention of visiting Paradise, but since they deemed some excuse necessary, they had had recourse to this weak one.

In days of old when knights were bold it is possible that two young men setting out on a similar errand would have endeavored to find the shortest possible distance between themselves and their destination, and have hewed to that line.

Such was not Flash McCarroll's way. By no chance would he have had Frazier Thane think that he had set out with the deliberate intention of calling on her. To follow the road that led from the Lazy K past the Thane place and on to town was not to be thought of either, for that promised only a passing nod of recognition, since one was either going to town or was not.

The result of all this was that Flash and Lin were no sooner out of sight of the ranch-house than they swung far to the north and east, describing a great circle that finally brought them back to the Paradise road several miles east of the Thane place. Now, to all appearances, they were returning from town, and if, by chance, they should meet the object of their reconnaissance they would feel at liberty to tarry indefinitely, since one can always go home.

It so happened that the young lady, who was their chief concern that pleasant afternoon, was in a most trying predicament at the time.

Frazier's uneasiness had grown as the afternoon wore on. Despite Chris Bridger's vehement warning, she refused to believe that her father might be attacked on the way home. And yet she decided at last to saddle her mule, her only means of travel when her father was using their horse, and ride toward town, hoping to meet him this side of the Reserve.

She had named the mule Horace Greeley — mainly because the animal had ideas of his own which he took the most inopportune times to assert. But Horace had his virtues; he was tireless and long-suffering.

This afternoon he had seemed more tractable than usual, and Frazier had covered almost the entire distance from the ranch to the line of the Reserve without mishap of any sort. She had seen nothing of her father, however. The sun was still high, and she resolved to ride on for a time, at least.

When she had entered the Reserve for the distance of about a mile, she came to Emigrant Creek. Because it was always fordable, save for a few days in early spring, no one had ever thought of bridging it.

Horace rolled his eyes at sight of the water — this was usually a sign that he and Frazier were about to disagree. Being forewarned, she sought to urge him across the creek before he had time to fully make up his mind to the contrary.

Her promptness did gain her a few feet, but in the middle of the stream Horace caught up with his mental processes and decided he was not going across.

Frazier began by coaxing him and gradually advanced through all the wiles of persuasion that she thought Horace might be susceptible to until she ended in sheer exasperation.

She belabored him with her heels, but Horace budged not. So there she sat, marooned in midstream and not knowing whether to laugh or cry.

When forty minutes had passed and Horace still refused to either retreat or advance, Frazier could no longer summon a smile to her lips. Dull red spots of anger burned in her cheeks, and with determination born of desperation, she removed her shoes and was about to do the same with her stockings when Lin and Flash appeared, apparently out of nowhere.

Lin took in the situation at a glance and laughed. Flash gave him a dig in the ribs.

"You danged fool, what you laughin' about?" he demanded. "Can't you see she's in distress?"

Lin could see nothing but Frazier, trying desperately now to hide her stockinged feet in her stirrups. Under his breath he muttered, "Your brain is addled, Flash, but your eyes is sure OK!"

Frazier had overheard Flash's remark, and now that help was at hand, she found it possible to smile over it. She flushed slightly as she became aware of the amused interest of the lean, bronzed and altogether handsome man to whom Flash had addressed himself. Lin smiled, then, a shy little wistful smile that made her catch her breath.

She knew she must appear ridiculous, perched there on the back of Horace Greeley. Lin thought her adorable, but Frazier bit her lips in embarrassment and asked herself why she hadn't waited another five minutes before starting to disrobe.

Unconsciously she wriggled her toes. Lin saw, and laughed aloud. Instantly she knew why he laughed. Flash glared at his friend.

"Don't pay no attention to him, Miss Frazier," he called out. "He ain't really what'd you'd call right." He was uncoiling his rope. Lin stopped him as he started across the creek.

"If you put a rope on that mule he'll sit down, like as not," he drawled pleasantly. "Piñon will haze him out of there in a hurry. You hang on, Miss. My horse is an old hand at this trick."

Lin's knees sank into Piñon's glossy sides and the horse moved into the creek. Horace Greeley rolled his eyes at him as if scenting trouble. He braced his rear legs noticeably and stretching out his neck, swung his gaunt head around farther and farther with every step Piñon took until his muzzle almost touched the saddle.

"He's watchin' yuh!" Flash called. "Look out for him."

Lin nodded. "Now, Piñon, *take* him!"

Piñon's nostrils dilated. The next instant his jaws closed over Horace Greeley's right hindleg. A wolf hamstrings an elk or deer in exactly the same fashion.

42

Horace forgot to kick. He squealed wildly instead, and hunching himself, leaped almost to the bank in a single bound.

"You *can* move, can't yuh?" Flash exclaimed dryly, catching the reins from Frazier as Lin rode up and helped her out of the saddle.

"Hope you didn't get shook up too much," Lin apologized.

"No, I'm quite all right," said she. "A little persuasion does wonders, doesn't it?"

"All depends where it's applied," Flash cut in. "This is my friend Lin Kincaid."

Frazier nodded graciously. "It is a pleasure to meet any friend of Mr. McCarroll," said she.

It was the first time in years that Flash had been addressed as mister, and he swelled out with new importance, even if he had cause to wonder where Lin had learned to bow so gracefully. In a desperate attempt to show Frazier that he was no mean cavalier himself, he squared his shoulders and figuratively closing his eyes for the fatal plunge, exclaimed:

"Might I assist you with your shoes, Miss Frazier?"

Frazier had to bend over quickly that Flash might not catch the merry twinkle in her eyes. "No, thanks," she managed to say, "I'll be just a second."

Lin had less consideration for Mr. McCarroll, and he turned on him and shook his head pityingly. "You old fool!" said Lin's eyes. "You won't live this down if you get to be a hundred."

"I suppose you were on your way to town," Lin queried a moment later.

Frazier explained that she had come this far hoping to meet her father.

"If you go on," Lin advised, "you may have trouble gettin' across here on your way home. It'll be growin' dark in another hour."

"I think I'll turn back now," she decided, "if Horace is agreeable."

"Horace?" chuckled Flash. "I claim that mule is most appropriately named."

"As long as Piñon is here he won't give you any trouble, ma'am," Lin declared. "Try it now."

When Frazier was seated, Lin whispered to his horse. Piñon snorted. That was enough for Horace Greeley.

"You talk to that horse as though he were human," she said as they rode away from the creek.

"He *is* just about human," Lin drawled. "Leastwise he savvys human talk. He was runnin' wild on the range when I put my rope over him for the first time. We been together a while since then."

Modest, unassuming Lin filled Frazier with a strange agitation. Frazier made him admit he was rather good at breaking horses.

Flash insisted that Lin was the best bronc peeler in that country. This drew a dissenting shake of the head from Kincaid.

"Mebbe you're a miner, then," Flash flung back at him. "He actually did have a mine once on Emigrant Creek."

"Yes?"

44

"The only thing the matter with it was that the gold along the creek had been nipped by the frost or somethin' that year and didn't come up."

Frazier was enjoying herself immensely. Time passed quicker than she realized, and before long they came in sight of home.

Flash was still at his usual game of trying to exasperate Lin into argument. Lin's sense of humor was deep and abiding, and Flash was more often at his mercy than he suspected.

For Lin could turn a countenance as guileless as a babe's on the victim he had selected and by his very innocence and seeming sincerity lure the unhappy wretch to most ridiculous lengths. Ever since leaving the creek Flash had taken keen delight in raking up Lin's past and making him miserable. Lin struck back now, and without mercy.

"I reckon Miss Thane ain't never heard no real cowboy songs back east where she comes from, Flash," he declared. "I bet she'd admire to hear you sing one or two."

"Oh, naw!" Flash exclaimed, although he would rather sing than eat, if the result he achieved might properly be called singing. People who heard him once remembered him forever.

"Don't tell me you sing?" Frazier exclaimed inocently, playing Lin's game to perfection.

Flash bowed his head sheepishly. "I warble a little," he admitted.

"Oh, you *must* sing, then! What will it be?"

"Don't make much difference to me," he declared, "I know 'em all." He fished out a mouth-organ and played a tune. "This is a pretty good one. It's called 'Jesse James.' It goes like this:

"Jesse James was a lad that killed a-many a man;
He robbed the Danville train.
But that dirty little coward that shot Mr. Howard
Has laid poor Jesse in his grave.
Poor Jesse had a wife to mourn for his life;
Three children, they were brave,
But that dirty little coward that shot Mr. Howard
Had laid poor Jesse in his grave."

There was much more; this was but the beginning, and Flash struggled manfully with every line of it. Frazier had to look away. As she turned her head she surprised the amused look in Lin's gray eyes and understood what he was about.

"Don't you think he ought to have a voice like that trained?" Lin inquired of her when Flash ended all out of breath.

"Training could hardly improve it," Frazier declared.

"Well, there's somethin' in what you say," Lin admitted, very deep now.

"Shucks!" Flash gasped, pulling at his hat in his embarrassment. "It ain't really that good is it?"

Frazier hesitated, and Lin answered for her. "You're only fishin' for compliments," said he. "Do you want it in writin'? Go on and sing!"

Without thinking, Flash favored them with "Jack Austin," in the fourth stanza of which Jack falls in love with a sheep-herder's daughter and is ostracized as a result.

This song was as lugubrious and senseless as such ballads usually are, but it rubbed the smile from Frazier's lips. Too late, Flash realized his blunder. Lin caught his eye and stopped him from making matters worse by trying to explain.

All three, Frazier especially, realized that although this was the first time sheep had been mentioned that evening, it was a subject that could not be avoided, and, for her part, one that she saw no reason to avoid.

They reached the house a few minutes later. Frazier gave them her hand, thanking them for rescuing her and for the very pleasant ride home.

"I hope you will not be strangers," she smiled. "It has been a rather thrilling day for me. Mr. Bridger and Mr. Cantrell called this afternoon."

"Did they?" Lin asked, and his drawl had suddenly deepened. "Crowdin' you a little, I suppose?"

"Well — they seemed quite disturbed over Father's decision to go in for sheep. But I hope matters can be adjusted to the satisfaction of all."

"That is brave talk, ma'am," Lin said slowly. "You let me know if they ride you too hard. You've got some friends, even if they are on the other side."

"You're right, Lin!" Flash exclaimed. "We're only workin' for Cantrell; he ain't got our vote yet."

"What? You ride for Mr. Cantrell?" Frazier demanded quickly. "Oh, but of course — the Lazy K. I should have known."

She found it difficult to hide her disappointment. It was an unhappy ending to the pleasantest hours she had known since coming West.

Lin and Flash turned in their saddles and waved good-night as they rode away. Neither spoke for a time. It was Flash who broke silence first.

"Ain't I stupid?" he growled. "Singin' that fool song. Why didn't you kick me, Lin?"

"No sense walkin' around things like that," said sober-faced Lin. "I wish I could figure a way out for her. I'm afraid there ain't none."

CHAPTER
FIVE

The Tree of Hate

Twilight was gone by the time they reached Cottonwood Creek. Piñon was halfway across when Lin felt him stiffen. Flash's horse stopped too and threw up his head with ears erect and nostrils dilated.

"What's up?" Lin exclaimed.

"Bob-cat or coyote, like as not," Flash answered. "Somethin' on the ground over there. See it?"

Lin nodded and was about to urge Piñon ahead when he thougth he heard some one groan off to his right. His hand flashed to his gun. Flash saw him go taut. "What is it?" he whispered.

"Listen!"

The sound was repeated. The two men looked at each other.

"Humph!" Flash muttered. "It came from the other side of the creek."

"Who is it?" Lin called.

There was no answer. They listened again and once more the night wind brought to their ears the low groaning of someone evidently in great pain.

"Where are you?" Lin cried. He had forced Piñon across the creek. There was no answering call. "Light a match, Flash!"

Flash broke off a piece of dry sage and set fire to it. "My God," he cried as he saw the slaughtered sheep, "been trouble here!"

Lin swung to the ground and made a flambeau of his own. He had moved down the creek only a few yards when he caught sight of young Cèsar. The boy lay as Cantrell and Bridger had left him.

Flash ran to Lin's side. Their faces were white. Here was the bloody beginning of the fight that both had feared would come.

Flash recognized the boy. "He's been layin' here two or three hours by the look of things."

"I'm afraid he's dyin'," Lin muttered. "Get some water, Flash."

Cèsar's eyelids fluttered open as Lin bathed his face. Lin was a stranger. When he saw Flash, however, he recoiled, for he knew McCarroll was a Lazy K man.

"I ain't goin' to hurt you," Flash exclaimed sharply. "What you drawin' away from me for?"

"Wait," said Lin. "I think I understand. Can't you put two and two together?"

Flash drew in his breath sharply. "Oh — h!" he exclaimed pointedly. "So that's it — Cantrell!"

Lin did not answer but asked the boy what had happened.

Cèsar shook his head, afraid of further injury.

50

"Why didn't you stay where you belonged?" Flash scolded. "You been warned and put off and God knows what — but you wouldn't learn."

"You don't have to be afraid; we ain't goin' to hurt you," Lin remarked. "How long you been here?"

"Long time," the boy murmured. His voice was very faint.

"Well, you tell us just what happened," Lin pursued. "You got caught over here with your sheep; did you refuse to get out?"

"My sheep got across while I fall asleep. First I knew ees when I hear gun shoot."

Gradually Lin got out of him a detailed story of what had occurred.

"You're certain it was Cantrell that shot you, eh?" Lin asked a second time.

"It was Cantrell, *Señor*," Cèsar answered. "Tell my grandfather."

"There'll be trouble enough without that," Flash growled. Lin called him aside.

"What are we going to do with him?" he asked. "I reckon he won't live long, but we can't leave him here. I've bandaged him up the best I know how."

"Can we take him to the valley?"

"He'd never reach there alive. If he's going to have a chance we'd better try the Thane place. Maybe she'll be able to do somethin' for him."

"I reckon she's game enough to try."

Lin got into his saddle. "You hand him up to me, Flash. Soon as we get goin', you ride ahead and tell her to get things ready."

51

Flash was careful, but even so, the boy groaned as the red-haired one lifted him up. Lin rode slowly, holding him in his arms. Cèsar's pulse became fainter and fainter until Lin was uncertain whether he lived or not.

Frazier and Flash were waiting for him when he rode into the yard. "Better take him in the kitchen, I guess," said he.

"This is terrible," Frazier exclaimed. "Is he still alive?"

"I ain't certain."

Flash carried Cèsar into the kitchen and placed him on the floor. He shook his head as he got to his feet. "I'm afraid he's gone," he muttered.

"He's such a boy!" Frazier cried, her eyes misty.

Lin made a hurried examination. "Yes, he's dead all right," they heard him murmur.

He asked Frazier to get something to cover the boy.

"What'd you tell her?" Lin asked Flash.

"Not much. Just that we had found him and that some of his sheep had been killed."

Lin nodded slightly. "Better not say too much." Frazier came back presently. Lin glanced at her. She was crying softly. "It's pretty bad," said he; "but I reckon it had to come."

Frazier whirled on him.

"Why do you take it for granted that this boy had to be killed? I don't know what you call it, but it is nothing less than murder to me."

Her eyes were cold and challenging as they met Lin's. He felt the rebuke, even accusation they carried, for in Frazier's mind there had been born the awful suspicion that Lin and Flash knew more than they were telling.

"When you know this country better and get a proper idea of the fight that is goin' on for it, I reckon you won't have to ask," he explained. "I only hope nothin' like this happens to you folks."

Frazier winced at the thought, but her courage did not desert her. "I think there is little likelihood of that; we are not Basques to suffer in silence and retaliate when the opportunity comes. Is it possible no effort will be made to bring to justice the man or men who killed this boy?"

"I'm afraid there won't be much done about it," Lin declared miserably. "It's happened before."

"That is why it continues to happen. Certainly you and Mr. McCarroll have some idea of who committed this crime."

Flash tried to exchange a furtive glance with Lin. Frazier caught him, and despite her better judgment, she became more suspicious than ever.

"It ain't usually healthy to express opinions in such matters," Lin said evasively. He was only being true to the code of the range and the only life he had ever known. If Cantrell were turned over to the law to-morrow he would not raise a hand to save him. He drew his wages from Big Jim, and although that made a certain sense of loyalty obligatory, he was, in most things, a free agent.

"But you *do* know," Frazier drove on persistently. "You must have found some clue. This boy was harmless. He had come here several times. In fact it was he who suggested that Father see his grandfather about a herder. His brother, Bonafacio, has been with him right along. Why, it was only about noon to-day that Bonafacio passed here. I was outside at the time. He said he was going home. You must have passed him coming up from Paradise. What time did you leave town?"

Flash twirled his hat uneasily. Why had he used that lie to her? Lin was hardly less worried. "Ma'am," said he, stung to frankness, "we hadn't been to town as we said."

Frazier's heart sank. Was it possible that they were the guilty ones?

"But you are dressed for town. Why did you say you were returning from the valley?"

That could not be answered either. Lin's face was tense and white. He stared deep into Frazier's eyes for seconds before he spoke. "Ma'am," he began awkwardly, "I hope you ain't thinkin' we had anythin' to do with this."

Flash's mouth sagged open and as he glanced from Lin to Frazier and back to Lin, his eyes slowly widened. This deduction had quite escaped him.

"I don't want to think you had," Frazier answered, her voice breaking.

"Don't think that," Flash cried. "We'd hardly have brought him here if we'd been mixed up in this."

"Unless you were clever enough to figure that would be the best way to throw suspicion away from you," said a voice from the doorway.

54

Lin wheeled on his heels to find himself facing a white-haired man of sixty.

"Father!" Frazier cried. "What a fright you gave me! How long have you been standing there?"

"Long enough to understand what has happened. You seem to be acquainted with these men. Will you explain?"

Frazier did that easily enough. Lin and Flash bowed stiffly to old Aaron. He recognized the introduction with an almost imperceptible nod. "Where did the boy die?" he demanded.

"Somewhere between Cottonwood Creek and here," said Lin.

"I don't suppose you could prove that he wasn't dead before you left the creek?"

"It'd be pretty difficult to prove that," Lin admitted.

"I suppose the coroner will be interested in that."

"The coroner won't get very excited about this affair," said Flash. "I reckon this boy's people won't insist on anythin' like that."

"Well, it's their right," Aaron exclaimed, bristling belligerently.

Kincaid shook his head a little pityingly. "I wouldn't get too excited about their rights," he declared; "they haven't lost sight of many of them since they been in this country. The thing to do now is to decide what we're goin' to do with the boy. We can't take him back where we found him and leave him to the coyotes, and it ain't fair to you folks to leave him here."

"There's two Basque boys out in my barn now," Aaron volunteered. "One of them is working for me;

the other just helped us home and was going back in the morning. If you want to take the responsibility, I'll loan you my horse and wagon. Maybe you could get this boy Francisco to make the trip."

"I don't mind the responsibility," said Lin. "If the boy won't go, I will."

They placed the body in the wagon before consulting the boys.

"I smell sheep," Flash muttered under his breath as he and Lin walked to the barn. Aaron was just ahead of them. "There they are, too," Flash added a moment later. "He's stuck to his word. I wonder what Big Jim will say to that."

The Basque boys became wildly excited as Aaron acquainted them with what had occurred. Francisco was not anxious to make the long trip to the valley by night with such a load, even though he had known the dead Cèsar.

Loneliness and utter solitude they accepted without protest, and though fearless in many ways, they were so much the prey of superstition that the dead filled them with terror.

Esteban. Aaron's herder, was the more panic-stricken of the two. His face was ghastly in the lantern light.

Aaron asked Francisco finally if he would go if he allowed Esteban to accompany him. Lin had hoped they might speak in Spanish, which he could follow after a fashion. But as usual with the Basque at such moments, they raised the barrier of their racial language, and safe behind it, argued the matter until Esteban said they would go together.

Just as they were about to drive away, Lin put his hand on Esteban's shoulder and spoke to him rapidly in Spanish. Aaron did not like it, evidently fearing that Lin might be trying to intimidate the boy. Had the conversation continued, Aaron would have protested, but with the boy's answer, Lin waved them on their way. "I was just warning him," he explained when they had gone, "that you were countin' on him to come back. He promised he'd come."

"You don't think he would desert me, needing him as I do?" Aaron asked, far from mollified over what he felt had been a slight to him.

"That's exactly what he was plannin' to do. He promised to return in the mornin'. He won't come back until he's talked to his people. That's the Basque way."

Aaron let on that he was not worried. "He'll come back all right."

Lin sensed that they were not wanted. "Come on, Flash," he said.

They rode away without another word. Passing the house, both men looked for Frazier, but she was not to be seen.

"I guess she's pretty much upset," Flash volunteered.

"I reckon so," said Lin.

For some reason conversation died as they rode along. They had passed the creek before Flash asked Lin what he thought of Aaron.

"He's gettin' off to a bad start, worryin' about other people's rights," Lin exclaimed. "He's got troubles enough of his own, if he only knew it. He ain't goin' to make it any easier for her."

Flash was of the same opinion.

Although it was late by the time they rode into the Lazy K yard a light still burned in Cantrell's office. He came to the door and called as they rode past. "That you, Kincaid? You and McCarroll come in here a minute before you turn in."

It was evident he had been waiting up for them. He was in an unpleasant mood.

"Where you boys been?" he demanded without further ado.

Flash had entered first. "Why, we were just out takin' a little jaunt," he answered a little stiffly, not liking either Cantrell's tone or question.

"As a matter of fact, you were over to the Thane place makin' eyes at the daughter, weren't yuh, Kincaid?"

Flash turned his head so he could see Lin. "I reckon what I do and where I go when my work is finished is pretty near my own personal affair," Lin drawled, which in itself was usually a bad sign with him. "For another thing, sir, I ain't in the habit of makin' eyes at a lady."

Here was a challenge if Cantrell wanted to take it up. Flash saw his eyes narrow to mere slits. But Big Jim had no desire to lose a top hand just then. "That's war talk," said he, "but I'm goin' to overlook it, Kincaid. I won't even insist that you'd flirt, but I am goin' to tell yuh that I don't want my men sympathizin' with any

58

sheep-herder's family. It ain't goin' to be possible for anyone to straddle the fence in what's comin'."

He walked around to his desk and lit a cigar before sitting down. "That goes for you and all — *What's that!*" he broke off sharply, his eyes dilating strangely as he pointed at Lin.

Flash had stepped aside and Lin now stood facing Cantrell. His shirt was soaked with blood.

"Is that blood?" Big Jim demanded.

"I reckon it is. We found that herder."

"What herder?"

Lin made no effort to answer. Their eyes met, however, and it drew a smothered "Oh!" from Cantrell.

There was a world of expression in the simple exclamation. Cantrell smoked in silence. "What'd you do with him?" he asked at last.

"Took him over to the Thane place." Lin explained what they had done. "He wasn't dead when we found him," he added.

Big Jim placed his cigar on the desk with elaborate care and bent over and fixed his eyes on Kincaid. "Did he talk any?"

"He talked considerable."

"Oh!"

Cantrell was not wasting words now. "How much did *you* tell?" he inquired coldly.

He fidgeted nervously under the quiet contempt that crept into Kincaid's eyes.

"Nothing," said Lin. It was no compliment to him that Cantrell found the question necessary.

"That's right, sit tight; this will either bring those fools to their senses or tear things wide open." Cantrell got out a box of cigars and a bottle. "Have a drink," he insisted as he found the glasses.

"No, I ain't drinkin'," Lin drawled. Flash was not so abstemious.

They spoke for a minute about the horses that were being broken. Cantrell walked to the door with them. "Good-night," he called after them.

There was no answering sign from Lin. Big Jim's lips curled scornfully.

"You wonder what you know, don't you?" he muttered when they were gone. "Don't you git too big, young fellow; I may trim your wings yet!"

CHAPTER
SIX

The Tree Bears Fruit

Cantrell knew that news of Cèsar's death would spread rapidly in the valley. Accordingly he sent his foreman to town the following evening to feel the public pulse. It was after midnight when Uncle Henry returned to the Lazy K. His expression was so serious that it was hardly necessary to ask him what he had learned.

"They're takin' it mighty hard," said he. "There was a big crowd in Benavides' saloon. They knew I was there and they stepped on me pretty strong. All I had to do was ask for trouble and I'd had a big order of it."

"We've heard 'em talk before," Cantrell replied with more confidence than he actually felt. "I'm glad this thing got under their skins. Maybe they'll change their minds about applying for permits."

Uncle Henry shook his head. "I wouldn't count on it," said he. "Irquieaga and his crowd are only waitin' for the funeral to be over; we'll hear from 'em for certain, and old Angel won't stop 'em. There's been a regular procession over to Angel's *caserio* to-day. He's counseling them to go slow."

"There you are! He knows where he heads in at. There ain't any fight in him."

"That isn't what the record says," Hank declared flatly. "Don't you make any mistake about him not bein' able to fight."

"You seem to think pretty well of him," Cantrell snapped.

Uncle Henry was unruffled by Cantrell's tone. "I don't underestimate him," said he. "But there's some of the Basques feel like you do about him — Ramon Irquieaga and his crowd, for instance. If old Angel don't act, Irquieaga will; he's just dyin' to show his people that he ought to be their leader."

Cantrell knew Irquieaga — a burly man of forty who had first attracted attention to himself by his wrestling. He had been a thorn in Angel Irosabal's side for years, their quarrel having begun over the adjudication of water rights on Martins Creek in the Basques' first great struggle to make the state recognize their claims. Irquieaga always contended that their leader had failed them in agreeing to compromise the matter, taking half a loaf when he might have had a whole one.

"Irquieaga can have all the trouble he wants," Cantrell said evilly. "He don't worry me a bit."

"Just the same I'm goin' to get ready for him," said Uncle Henry. "Unless I'm an old fool we can expect him one of these nights."

Bridger arrived at the Lazy K early in the afternoon of the following day. Cantrell had sent for him. "What do you hear?" was his first question.

"They're turned inside out, according to Hank. The funeral is this afternoon. I'm goin' to send somebody down to have a look."

"It's invitin' trouble. Adams and Wheeler (both cattlemen) were over to see me early this mornin'. They're worried about this. Wheeler said it wasn't the right way to handle things."

"How'd he handle them?" Cantrell thundered. "They don't know what's what (this was accompanied by a knowing wink) do they?"

"Do you think I'm crazy?" Bridger demanded, his face purpling.

"Well, two of my men know," Big Jim admitted. "Kincaid and McCarroll got the whole affair before that damned bosko kicked out."

Although the papers on Cantrell's desk rustled in the breeze that had been blowing all day, Bridger suddenly found the day warm. "My God," he muttered, more to himself than Cantrell, and then repeated it. "What you goin' to do?" he asked, hitching his chair nearer Cantrell's.

"Nothin'," Big Jim answered crisply — "not for the present, I mean. In a pinch, I could handle McCarroll. I don't know about Kincaid; he's got a ramrod up his back right now."

"Why?"

"Oh, he's got his eye on that Thane girl. I told him to keep away, and he didn't like it a bit."

Old Chris whistled. "Say!" he warned, "this is serious. He ain't afraid of nothin'. He had the reputation of bein' a wildcat in a fight over where he came from. He won't bluff worth a cent. If you make a move, be prepared to go through with it. I'd like it better if he was out of this altogether."

"But I'm not ready to admit it is goin' to amount to anythin'. If it does and he starts to kick over the traces, I reckon I'll know what to do. I was over to the Thane place again. Seems they kinda got the idea McCarroll and Kincaid might have had a hand in bumpin' off that kid."

This was interesting, and Bridger insisted on the details.

"I'd remember that," he said, stressing his words. "You may have to git rid of 'em in a hurry."

"You ain't tellin' me nothin'," Cantrell protested. "I may be able to make somethin' of that little lie of theirs. Come to think of it, I'll ask them to look things over this afternoon."

"I wouldn't! They're almost certain to git in a jam, especially if there's any suspicion that they had a hand in the trouble."

"I don't care if they do," Cantrell blustered.

"But don't you understand that if they are bein' suspected that it'll look mighty queer, them bein' in town to-day. If there's trouble, they may talk."

Cantrell would not be turned from his avowed intention. "If there's trouble it will be of their own pickin'. As for talkin' — I'll take a chance that they won't; you can't always play it safe."

Later on in the afternoon he made his wishes known to Flash. McCarroll found Lin and enlightened him. "I didn't hire out to do Cantrell's spyin'," Lin drawled. "He'll have to get someone else."

"Now don't fly off the handle that-a-way," Flash remonstrated. "Miss Frazier's old man went out of his way to let us know he didn't believe our story. If other folks has got the same idea, it wouldn't help us none to have it said that we refused to go to town to-day. I'd like to know just what the Basque *genté* is thinkin', anyway."

This argument swayed Lin, and they left a little after four o'clock. The Thane place seemed to be deserted as they passed.

"Gone to the funeral, like as not," Flash mused.

Lin nodded. "I was hopin' they wouldn't see the need of doin' that," said he.

There were stretches of the road which led down from Hinkey Summit which commanded an unobstructed view of the valley below. Flash pointed out the procession leaving the cemetery.

"Certainly gave the kid a great turn-out," he muttered. "The town will be full up when we get there. It'll be like walkin' on eggs to keep out of trouble."

Neither was armed. Both believed this slightly insured their safety.

Near the base of the Summit they saw a rig approaching. It was Frazier and her father.

Lin and Flash drew up at the side of the road and doffed their Stetsons. Old Aaron nodded his head about a quarter of an inch. Frazier smiled sadly. She had been crying.

"The temperature sure took an awful drop around here," Flash muttered as they rode on.

"It's got cool, to say the least," answered Lin.

On arriving in town, they went to the post office. The main street of Paradise Valley was only a block long. It was crowded with teams and rigs of one sort and another to-day.

They left their horses in front of the hotel, which was next door to Benavides' bar, a Basque stronghold. They had an old friend at the hotel in the person of Curly, the bartender. "Get out of town if you've got any sense!" that worthy warned them.

"But we're peaceable men," Flash grinned.

"Well this ain't no place for peaceable men," Curly insisted. "Some folks don't hesitate to say that you and Lin had a hand in this affair."

"I'd like to hear someone say it," Lin answered grimly.

Curly was a mine of information.

"You must know the man who bought out Jenkins — Thane is his name." Lin and Flash nodded. "Well, he's been down here fluttering around. Seems he thinks the Basques' fight is his. He's been tellin' them they ought to have the coroner. They got him up here before the funeral. He's stalling, of course, but there may be an investigation yet."

"Let her come," Lin exclaimed.

When they were ready to leave, Curly leaned over the bar. "You better let me loan you a gun," he whispered.

"Not a chance," Lin declared emphatically.

"You're the doctor. But say, don't crowd Irquieaga; he's out to make something of this little affair."

When they were outside again Flash asked Lin about the big Basque. "Of course he's dangerous," Lin admitted; "all windbags and cowards are."

66

They had not taken five steps before their presence in town was noted. They were suffered to pass in silence, but in more than one pair of eyes they felt the hatred and contempt that for the present no one dared to voice.

A dozen young Basques lounged in front of Benavides' place.

"Come on, we're goin' in here," Lin drawled. "I'm right interested now in hearin' the talk."

As they passed through the swinging doors one of the group ran across the street and disappeared in back of Ugarde's general store.

The saloon was packed. There had been loud talking, and although the entrance of Lin and Flash hushed voices in the very middle of words, the excited conversation of the previous minute could not be erased instantly, and it still reverberated in the smoky atmosphere of the long room.

Dead silence followed as Lin and Flash tried to find a place at the bar. No one moved aside to accommodate them. They found a place at last near the door. Benavides and One-Eyed Manuel, the Mexican who had been tending bar for Benavides for fifteen years, were not engaged at the moment, but neither made the least move to learn their wants.

Save for the two men behind the bar, every eye in the place was on them. "Well, Joe," Lin said, "do we get a drink or do we wait on ourselves?"

Benavides turned involuntarily and encountered Lin's gray eyes. He would have loved to refuse them, but something in those deep gray depths gripped him and he set out two glasses and a bottle.

Lin watched the crowd's changing expression in the large mirror which rested upon the back bar. The dark, scowling faces which it reflected became mirrors themselves in turn in which he saw chagrin and disgust chased away by rage and hatred.

It soon became apparent to Lin and Flash that the crowd's interest had become divided between them and the door.

"They've sent for Irquieaga," Flash muttered.

"I hope so," Lin drawled lazily. His tone did not fool Flash. He knew Kincaid was keenly alive to their danger.

"We'll go out of here fightin'," Flash mused.

"Not unless they bring the fight to us. You let me handle Ramon."

Suddenly the crowd ceased to grumble. Lin did not have to look in the mirror to know that Irquieaga had arrived.

The big man, he weighed not less than two hundred and twenty, ran his eye along the bar. A Basque just in back of Lin gave up his place to him. Irquieaga accepted without a word and pushed Lin out of the way as he stepped up to the bar.

His beefy face was ugly and pockmarked, round little eyes peeped out between mounds of flesh. He faced an opportunity made to his liking and he came determined to turn it to his advantage.

Flash saw the light in Kincaid's eyes change. Experience had taught Flash that it wasn't safe to elbow his friend as the big Basque had done.

The crowd held its breath. Over in the corner a man shivered. The thing he felt was colder than any wind.

"Let's have a drink!" Irquieaga growled, and spreading his arms upon the top of the bar deliberately knocked over Lin's glass.

Those who expected to see Lin fly into a blind rage were disappointed. Lin wheeled and tapped the big man's arm. "Was that an accident?" he asked without even raising his voice.

Lin was the taller of the two. Irquieaga gazed up at him now with an ugly sneer on his lips. "I'll let you decide that, you gringo!" he snarled.

Kincaid did not have to raise his voice now to make himself heard. "I didn't think you'd have nerve enough to speak to me that-a-way. I wasn't lookin' for trouble with you."

The Basque laughed loudly to impress his audience. "You never wanted any trouble with me!"

"No? You've got a pretty short memory, haven't you, Irquieaga? You want to think back about five years. I've always believed you got the smallpox that winter; that your cousin Salvator died and the only reason you didn't was because an unknown party by the name of Kincaid took care of you, other folks havin' urgent business elsewhere. You remember anythin' about all that?"

This was something that Lin had never mentioned to Flash.

Irquieaga had not expected to face this incident out of the past. For the moment he was without an idea — always a bad predicament for a bully.

It has been said that if you do a favor for a Basque you win the gratitude of all his people. The shuffling of feet and the low muttering which followed now was proof that the seed Lin had sowed had fallen on fertile soil. In the saloon at the time were many who swore allegiance to the headsman, Angel Irosabal. They were not opposed to seeing Irquieaga humbled.

"Why do you come here where you are not wanted?" the big man asked, trying to turn the conversation to a subject that promised more popular support.

"You haven't answered me yet, Irquieaga," Lin insisted quietly. "Is my memory at fault or is yours?"

"I remember all right," he answered fiercely. "I remember other things, too! You are the two who claim you found Cèsar, eh?"

The written words do not carry the insinuation he managed to put into them.

Kincaid's face paled a trifle. Only Flash surmised that a seething volcano lay just beneath that calm exterior.

"We don't *claim* we found him," Lin exclaimed pointedly. "Don't make that mistake again!"

Things were not going Ramon's way at all. He was angry with himself now. If he could only get his big hands and long arms around this gringo, matters could be settled quickly enough!

"Why didn't you leave him where you found him?" he made bold to ask in his mounting rage. "Since when do you people trouble yourselves over a Basque? How did it happen that you were crossing the creek that night? No one saw you in town that afternoon."

70

It dawned on Lin in a flash that he had Aaron Thane to thank for this. The old man had talked, and such talk at a time like this runs faster than the wind.

"Now I wait for you to answer," Irquieaga thundered.

Lin had no answer ready. Frazier Thane's name must not be brought into this.

"That's our affair," he exclaimed desperately. It was a lame excuse and sounded doubly so, voiced in the charged atmosphere of the crowded saloon.

Irquieaga's eyes flamed now. Things were going his way at last.

He backed away from the bar until he stood squarely before the swinging doors. "You'll answer before you get out of here," he snarled. "You'll answer now and we'll answer tonight!"

He had not meant to say so much, but he had lost his head completely.

"Get out of the way!" Lin murmured.

"Make me get out of the way!"

For answer Lin handed his hat to Flash. "Get ready," he whispered.

The giant saw him raise his hands to a fighting position. It was only a feint on Lin's part, for the next instant he dove head first into the Basque's stomach. As Lin butted him, the breath rushed out of Irquieaga in a great rumbling "W-h-o-o-s-h!"

He had not been prepared for such tactics. He flung out his hands to keep himself from falling, but the swinging doors gave way with him and he tumbled backwards and slid halfway across the sidewalk with a sickening groan.

"Quick!" Lin whipped out.

Flash was almost as good as his name for once. They were in their saddles before the crowd began to pour out of the saloon.

"Let's ride," Lin sang. "We won't have to bother about coming to town for a long while after this."

CHAPTER
SEVEN

An Eye for an Eye

At first it seemed they would be pursued. Two or three young men did take after them, but long before Lin and Flash reached the road which wound up to the top of Hinkey Summit, the pursuing riders turned back.

"I never knew your head was so hard," Flash laughed when they reined in their horses. "Curly was right; we shouldn't have gone into Benavides'."

"Why not? We got the information we went after. I reckon it slipped out unconsciously."

"You mean about to-night? Just talk, I thought."

"Well, we're warned, if that means anythin'. There seems to be a lot of talk — most of it done by a man who is makin' a terrible mistake."

"Meanin' Miss Frazier's father!"

Lin nodded, but did not speak at once. Flash waited for him to put his thought in words.

"Might ain't right, and I never said it was," Lin declared weightily at last. "But before a man goes to fussin' around in other folks' affairs and talkin' about rights, he ought to get acquainted with the country and its ways. He means well enough, but just look what he's done already. If any sense is to come out of this fight it's got to come through old Angel, as far as the Basque *genté* is concerned. Inflamin' blowhards like Irquieaga will only lead to more killin'."

"You don't think they can pin anythin' on us, do you?"

"Stranger things than that have been done. We had no reason for wantin' to get rid of that boy."

"None except that he was on one side and we're on the other." Flash answered solemnly. "That's reason enough in times like these."

Night had fallen before they reached the Thane ranch. A light burned brightly in the kitchen.

"When she hears, and she will, I hope she won't think we went to town just to pick trouble," Lin mused to himself. "There's nothin' I wouldn't do for her. I wish her father had half her sense."

He fell to dreaming. He knew there were few girls who would face the loneliness and problems that were hers without complaining. He could only surmise how great was the change her life had undergone.

There was something fine and gentle in her that he had found in no one else. It filled him with humbleness and made him freshly aware of his own shortcomings.

Later on they came to the creek where they had found Cèsar. Both unconsciously spurred their horses and were glad to leave the place behind.

Cantrell was waiting for them, as they knew he would be. Bridger was still there.

"Goin' to have the coroner, eh?" Big Jim smiled when he learned the news. "I'll believe that when it happens; the coroner knows who elects him."

Lin's story of his encounter with Irquieaga was brief and to the point. Cantrell seemed to enjoy it.

"Hank is ready for them," he exclaimed with his habitual cocksureness. "You boys turn in; you may be needed before the night is over."

Bridger and he sat for an hour discussing probabilities.

"Learned somethin' and didn't lose a thing by sendin' them in," Cantrell exclaimed as he summed up matters. "If we get pressed about that herder, little things like this trouble with Irquieaga will have more weight than you suspect."

He left Bridger alone and went upstairs to break open a case of ammunition. Chris seemed to doze in his chair, but he was really quite awake. He had remembered Cantrell's use of the pronoun "we." The more he thought of it, the less he liked it.

As the night wore on, Uncle Henry began sending out his men in pairs. It must have brought back memories of the old days when raids and rustlers were nightly occurrences.

At midnight, Lin and Flash were called. Cantrell and Bridger were going out, too. They went east, a mile north of the Thane place. Uncle Henry and Spike Dowd were immediately below them. Cantrell and Bridger were to station themselves to the north. Farther south, below Uncle Henry and Spike, were the others.

Every man was on the line by this arrangement, but they seemed a mere handful for all the eastern Lazy K frontier.

"Chances are this is all for nothin', but if they come, burn 'em good," was Cantrell's parting advice.

Flash was sleepy. He complained to Lin. "I bet Ramon is sittin' in Benavides' saloon laughin' to himself right this moment. If he could see us he'd git a stroke, like as not."

Lin did not deign to reply as they parted. He moved north and Flash went south. They were to continue on until they met the men above and below them, when they were to retrace their way and meet in the arroyo in which they had parted. This was to be kept up at regular intervals until daylight.

The night was darker than usual, and as Lin rode along he watched Piñon rather than the country about him. He knew he could trust to the horse where his own eyes were of little use.

When he had gone as far as he believed he should, he stopped, and swinging his foot over his saddle-horn, rolled a cigarette. He was about to light it when a faint halloo reached him. When it came a third time it was distinct enough for him to recognize the voice. It was Uncle Henry. Lin answered then.

"Why didn't you sing out?" Uncle Henry demanded.

"You're apt to lose your scalp that-a-way," Lin smiled. "You see anythin'?"

They talked easily. Uncle Henry had seen it all — free range to barbed wire. He had the cowman's traditional hatred for sheep. Lin believed the fact that the Lazy K was prosperous was due more to Uncle Henry than Cantrell.

The old man broke off in the middle of a sentence and jumped to his feet. Lin was right behind him. "What is it?" he whispered.

"Look!" Uncle Henry exclaimed. "Look at the sky! They've fired the ranch-house, sure as hell!"

To the west a crimson glow began to stain the heavens.

"We can't leave here," Lin declared. "They're hopin' this fire will draw us in, then they'll strike."

"You're right as usual!" Uncle Henry ground out. "She must be burnin' fast. Only Chang is there."

Cantrell and Bridger dashed up a few minutes later. Cantrell was beside himself.

"Stay here!" he shouted, hardly slackening the pace at which he rode. "Too late to save the house. We'll get out what we can. Give 'em hell, Hank!"

"We'll move north a bit," Uncle Henry suggested as Cantrell and Bridger galloped away.

They rode abreast, both wondering if all their personal effects had been destroyed. That was about the extent of their conversation.

As they came out of a dry wash Piñon stiffened and lifted his head. Lin reached out and grabbed the foreman's arm. "D'you hear it?" he cried.

"What?"

"Listen!"

A rifle shot, clear and distinct, broke the stillness of the night. It was followed almost immediately by another, and still another.

"They're in among our stuff!" Uncle Henry gasped. "They must have seen the boss pull out for home. Git your gun out and fan it. Let 'em know we're comin': it may bluff 'em out!"

They fired as they rode. When they reached the scene of the raid the enemy had flown, but there remained bountiful evidence of their work. The Lazy K paid dearly for the sheep that had been killed on Cottonwood Creek.

From one disaster, the men turned homeward to face another. Cantrell and Bridger met them before they reached the house. "Wasn't the house after all," he shouted, "just the haystacks!"

All sighed their relief.

"What are yuh comin' in for?" Big Jim demanded.

Uncle Henry told him. Cantrell went mad. He wouldn't hear to their turning in for the night.

Uncle Henry protested that it was unlikely that another attack would be made any more that night. He wanted the men fresh for the following night. Cantrell would not listen to him. "Get back where you were!" he fairly screamed. "You've got guns; show me that you know how to use 'em!"

True to Uncle Henry's prediction, the rest of the night passed without further trouble. Weary-eyed, they turned in at six o'clock. At eight, no less a person than Del Ryan, Humboldt County's political factotum and Cantrell's silent partner arrived.

Here was one man with whom Cantrell forgot to rant and bluster. The Honorable Del arrived in a temper. News of the raid and the firing of the hay did not help matters.

"What are you doin' here?" Cantrell asked uneasily.

"Time someone with a little sense got here," Del answered him. "I'm here to tell you there's going to be an investigation of this killing. The coroner will swear in a jury this noon at the Thane ranch."

"You mean it?"

"Do I ever kid you? You bet I mean it. I've seen Crocker; if it's possible he will hand down the usual verdict — 'by parties unknown.' Say — you know who bumped off that kid, don't you?"

Cantrell smiled inscrutably and leaned back in his chair. "Do I? Well, maybe I do. I wonder!"

CHAPTER
EIGHT

This is the Law!

The crowd gathered at the Thane ranch, arriving on horseback and in vehicles of every sort. The Basques came first, very solemn to-day in their Sunday black and stiff collars.

They bowed deferentially to Aaron, recognizing that he had championed their cause and forced the inquest which was to be held.

Aaron accepted their homage graciously. There was hardly a Basque present but knew of the raid on the Lazy K. By common consent, no one discussed the matter, even secretly. If they felt any apprehension as a result of it, it was well masked, and Aaron saw in them only a down-trodden people looking up to him for justice.

However, a little hush fell over the group as Irquieaga, attended by six of his most ardent supporters, rode into the yard. Knowing nothing of the raid, Aaron attached no importance to their coming. Frazier noted that they were heavily armed. Without knowing why, she took to watching them, and she soon sensed the suppressed excitement which their presence produced.

That Irquieaga was there was only because he was shrewd enough to know that to remain away was to indict himself with last night's attack.

Nate Crocker, the coroner, arrived then, and a few minutes later, Cantrell, Del Ryan and Bridger appeared, closely followed by Uncle Henry, Lin and Flash. In back of them followed four more Lazy K men.

Cantrell noticed Irquieaga immediately. His lean jaws snapped shut with the click of a steel trap. "Take it easy!" Del warned, prepared beforehand for such a moment.

The four Lazy K men who brought up the rear had no one to caution them. Unlike Lin and Flash, they followed Cantrell without question, and in the present instance asked for nothing better than a chance to square matters with Irquieaga.

The big Basque remained outwardly calm as they taunted and threatened him. But for Uncle Henry's watchfulness they would have been out of hand in another minute.

"Go slow, boys!" he muttered. "This score is goin' to be settled, and we'll take a little interest, too; but it ain't goin' to be done here to-day."

Cantrell and Bridger exchanged a rather anxious glance at finding themselves to be the only cattlemen present. "Where's Wheeler and the others?" he askd Chris. "They knew about this."

"They'll be here directly. It's early yet."

True to Bridger's prediction, they came shortly — Wheeler, both of the Adams brothers, Kent, Thad Taylor, Acklin — a dozen in all, and they arrived together! It said plainly enough that they had met somewhere by appointment.

"Been talkin' things over," Big Jim informed Chris. "Why did they leave us out?"

"I told you Wheeler didn't like the way things was goin'!"

Del was conferring with Aaron and the Coroner. He had advised Cantrell not to mention the raid to anyone; but in his resentment over what he termed plotting behind his back, Big Jim took matters into his own hands, and turned on his more wary neighbors with indignation and promptly acquainted them with what had occurred the past night.

The news had its effect. Cantrell smiled to himself as he saw their faces harden.

"They may be callin' on one of you to-night," he threw in for good measure. "It's a sample of what we've got to expect." He turned to the cautious Wheeler. "Maybe you figger we could *talk* 'em out of it?" he inquired with slightly veiled contempt.

They had drawn off to one side. Wheeler was not easily ruffled. "Talking will accomplish just as much as senseless killing," he shot back at Cantrell. "Here is the country all heated up about this boy being killed. While the excitement is going on, this man Thane brings in his sheep. Look at 'em! That's the thing we said wasn't going to happen."

They turned to stare at Aaron's flock, grazing on the slope that swelled away to the south. Each expressed his displeasure in his own way. "That's the thing that hurts!" Wheeler exclaimed. "If anyone ought to have felt the weight of our fist, Thane was the man."

"Don't you worry about him," Cantrell said deeply. "Just wait till things quiet down a bit."

The tension of the crowd increased as minutes passed and more cattlemen arrived. The line of cleavage was sharp; herders on one side of the yard, cowmen on the other. A little knot of men had gathered on the porch about the coroner. Nate Crocker was a brusque, self-centered individual, much given to oratorical rumbling and flag waving, ready at all times to impress his humblest constituent with his importance and the dignity of the humble office he had held so long.

The Basque *genté* was somewhat in awe of him. He represented the law — the very law that had shown them so little consideration in the past, but which to-day was being invoked in their behalf.

Nate had a trick of pulling out his immense watch and snapping it shut after a non-seeing glance that was quite effective. The inquest had been scheduled for twelve o'clock sharp, and although it still lacked fifteen minutes of that hour there were calls for him to begin. Nate's only answer was to flash his watch.

Del left the porch and crossed to where Cantrell and Chris stood talking to Wheeler and the others.

"What's he waitin' for?" Chris demanded.

"Angel Irosabal isn't here yet," replied Del.

"Well, I call that pretty good," someone laughed sarcastically.

"Just giving them a little taffy," Del explained. "He'll put Angel on the jury, and he'll be the only sheepman on it, too. It ain't necessary to have a unanimous finding; the majority will rule with Crocker."

Old Aaron found the coroner quite to his liking. They sat discussing politics now. Crocker was a silver Democrat. Back in his native habitat, Aaron had often proclaimed the the silverites were all consarned fools. He said nothing of the sort to-day. Indeed, under the persuasive eloquence of the solid citizen at his right, he was most pliable clay.

Somehow the issue no longer seemed such an important one. Here was a country to be settled. Men like Crocker were representative of the determined pioneers who were bringing law and justice to these remote frontiers and building a new and noble state out of the sagebrush wastes!

Of course these frontiers were no longer remote — if they constituted a frontier at all. The rangers in the National Forest were using aeroplanes to patrol it. There were telephones in some of the ranch-houses on Quinn River. Flivers were not unknown in the valley.

And yet, it was not Great Barrington, Massachusetts — not by many long miles! So Aaron can be forgiven his mistake. It is one common to tenderfoots.

The longer he listened to Nate the more convinced he became that Crocker was engaged in a work that he himself would be proud to have a hand in. An erroneous conclusion. And one, it may be added, that was not shared by Frazier Thane.

She found Crocker too shifty of eye, too flowery and altogether too anxious to please to be impressed by or even convinced of the man's integrity. She saw how the

Basques were impressed, however. The thought grew on her that this was only a show, arranged to appease them, and as the minutes passed and Crocker continued to turn his papers and snap his watch, she became almost certain of it.

She saw Lin and Flash arrive. She had been watching for them. Though she knew nothing about the raid, the first Basque to arrive had informed her of what had occurred in Benavides' saloon the previous afternoon. In the telling, Lin received none the best of it. It revealed him as being hand in glove with Cantrell and acting as the man's spy.

Be as charitable as she might, she could not help being displeased with him, and in turn with herself on finding how much it mattered to her. She had willed herself to put him out of her thoughts and had succeeded only to the extent of secretly watching for him to arrive. Now that he was here it pleased her to ignore him, without seeming to do so, and, when opportunity offered, to glance sharply at him as though she hoped to pierce his calm exterior and get at his real self.

Once she gazed too long. Lin caught her. He would have spoken in another moment, had she not succeeded in conveying the impression that her eyes were focused on some object far more distant than his unhappy self.

"She almost saw me that time," Lin muttered to Flash.

"She's been tryin' mighty hard not to see us ever since we rode in," Flash returned huffily. "We're about as popular around here as scarlet fever."

85

Lin made no reply. For the moment he was satisfied to know that she was concerned about him, even if negatively.

"I reckon she thinks we're a couple of horse-thieves," Flash growled, and turned away in search of the other Lazy K men.

Lin was not so easily vanquished. He was standing below the porch at the time. Surmising that Frazier, who had gone into the house, must soon come out again, he took himself around to the steps and found a place at the end of the porch opposite that occupied by Crocker and Aaron, where with a leg thrown carelessly over the railing he proceeded to roll a cigarette with the greatest deliberation.

It was hot on the porch. A few minutes later, Crocker called for a table and chair. When they were produced he had them carried out under the poplar trees to the right of the house.

"We'll get started soon," he announced, nodding toward an approaching rig. "Most likely that's Angel Irosabal coming now."

The opinion seemed to be shared generally and the crowd moved out under the trees. But not Lin! The door which led on to the porch opened almost at his elbow. If Frazier came out she would be face to face with him almost before she realized it.

So there he remained, determined to speak to her no matter what it cost.

CHAPTER
NINE

"You'll Marry Me Some Day"

He had not long to wait. Even as she opened the door he sprang to his feet and, hat in hand, bowed low with his usual grace.

Frazier's face flamed and she threw her head up haughtily. She divined at once that he had deliberately chosen this strategic spot so that she might not escape him. So she was not only disappointed with him, but displeased and now annoyed.

"Good-mornin', ma'am," Lin began easily enough. Gazing at her he found he had forgotten whatever it was that he had wanted to say, and he stood staring at her helplessly, his feet climbing over one another and appearing very little the gallant he so often seemed.

His confusion was so complete that Frazier had a difficult time preserving her superior manner. And yet he was not one to quit. He had something to say, and while he had hoped to say it less abruptly than must be the case now, still it must be said.

"I've been tryin' to see you ever since I rode in," he began stiffly.

"So you took this means of succeeding, I see," Frazier said icily, suddenly resolved to make him as miserable as she might.

Had she known her man better she would have hardly dared as much. His embarrassment was gone. In its place had come something that filled her with misgiving.

"I reckon I had to, ma'am," he murmured, "seein' you was determined not to see me."

Frazier had thought to unbend, but at this boldness she drew herself up more haughtily than ever. "Back where I come from, gentlemen do not force their attentions on a lady," she informed him with just that shade of emphasis that a woman always reserves for the man whom she admires most.

Lin staggered under this broadside. "I didn't mean to presume. I guess I'd better go."

Of course she did not want him to go. She had liked Lin from the first. It was not part of her plan to let him know it, however.

"You might have respected my wishes if you thought I was trying to avoid you," she countered. Lin remarked that she did not tell him to go. It made him bold.

"You didn't try to avoid me the other day at the creek."

Frazier caught her breath. "I don't think I shall ever like you," she exclaimed. "You are almost impudent. Anyhow, it was Piñon that rescued me!"

Lin found her more adorable than ever.

"My horse did have somethin' to do with it," he drove on; "I beg his pardon. As for never likin' me —

ma'am, I wouldn't worry about that. I've been promisin' myself that you'll marry me some day."

Frazier laughed — such a laugh as reduces a man to dust. It was more convincing than any denial that words could have framed.

"You are more amusing than I thought, Mr. Kincaid. So you have been promising yourself — for all of two days — that I would marry you! Even as devoted as you have been it has not seriously interfered with your *work*, I know."

The peculiar stress she placed on his work gave Lin his cue.

"I don't mind you bein' amused," said he; "there ain't much around here that is real downright amusin'. As for my work — as you call it — well, maybe I can guess what's on your mind. If there's any talk of my havin' anythin' to do with killin' that herder, you know where it started. If I thought you believed that, you'd never see me again."

"I don't believe it!" Frazier exclaimed earnestly. "No more would I have believed you capable of turning spy and riding into town seeking trouble before that boy was cold in his grave. But apparently I was mistaken."

Lin winced beneath the gall and wornwood of her contempt, he fought to keep back the hot words that rushed to his tongue.

"Folks who know me would hesitate to use that word to me, ma'am," he said finally. "I owe it to myself to keep my honor clean. Your father had no cause to put suspicion on me. He don't know me or this country.

89

I'm on one side of this fight and he's on the other. So it was natural for him to jump to the wrong conclusion.

"Cantrell asked me to go to town. Knowin' how your father felt and bein' sure he would talk, could I say no to Cantrell and have it get out that I refused to go to town? That man Irquieaga and his friends would have swore that I was afraid to go, which would have been just another way of sayin' that I was the guilty man."

Frazier could not admit that her father had been hasty, even though she felt it. It was hardly less difficult for her to insist that Lin had not justified his conduct. And yet, she could not allow him to win so easily.

"So to prove that you were innocent you went into that Basque saloon looking for trouble, eh?" she suggested with cutting irony.

Lin shook his head. "I've always gone into Benavides' place since I been in this country. Not to go in yesterday was to say I dassent. I had to show 'em I wasn't afraid to go where the talk was the worst. I owed that to myself."

"If you had stayed out they would have called you a coward — I take it that is what you are trying to say," Frazier taunted him.

"Somethin' like that," Lin muttered, consumed with resentment but unable to tear himself away.

"So you went in and proved that you were not a coward," she exclaimed sweetly. "You have been in this country long enough for men to know what you are. I fancy they do! It was not necessary for you to quarrel with that man to prove your courage."

Frazier had melted to tenderness.

"He brought the fight to me — and it wasn't really a fight," Lin insisted doggedly. "I don't know where you got your information, but if you got it all and got it straight, you know that Irquieaga is an ingrate. He was out to get me. They sent for him to make certain we'd meet. I don't want to offend you. Your good opinion means more to me than anythin' in the world."

"That's a very pretty speech, Mr. Kincaid," Frazier smiled. Strangely enough she had the feeling that she was hearing the truth.

"Most people call me Lin," said he, suddenly finding the distant hills very interesting.

"Well, Lin, promise me you will not carry this fight any farther." She was utterly appealing now.

"Don't make me lie to you," he begged. "Irquieaga raided us last night, firin' our hay and killin' a lot of stock."

Frazier gasped her surprise.

"We knew there was a fire somewhere over west!" she exclaimed. "Once I thought I heard shooting."

"There was plenty of it." He gave her the details.

"What a way, what a stupid way to go about settling this trouble! Now there will be reprisals, more raids!"

Lin nodded soberly. "I don't want to alarm you, but I'm sure that's bound to happen. And it won't always end like it did last night. So don't ask a promise of me that I can't keep. But remember this, I don't aim to do anythin' that would shame me in your eyes." He paused for a moment and his wistful smile came back. "You rode me pretty hard this mornin'," he drawled.

Lin's back was to the crowd and he did not see Cantrell approaching. Frazier saw him, however, and hurried her answer. "You rode beautifully," said she. "Here comes Mr. Cantrell."

Big Jim had been an interested witness of the scene on the porch. Bridger first called Cantrell's attention to her and Lin.

"Your fifty dollar a month cowpuncher is beatin' yore time," Chris laughed aloud.

"He's got his rope on the wrong mare this time," Big Jim replied ominously.

To see them so well acquainted embittered him; and yet, for all his blustering he suffered ten minutes to pass before he walked toward the porch.

"Good-mornin', Miss Thane," he exclaimed warmly, ignoring Lin.

Frazier returned his greeting with noticeable reserve. She found Cantrell forbidding. She did not intend to have Lin snubbed by his boss. So it was with malice aforethought that she turned to Kincaid and exclaimed, "Why, you're not going, Lin?"

Lin had made no move to go, but he understood her instantly. "I reckon I'll drift down to the crowd. Things will be startin' right away."

Cantrell had not failed to note that she called him Lin. She need not have called him by name to convey her interest in him; her tone alone did that.

Frazier saw Cantrell's eyes snap. She knew she had succeeded better than she expected.

"Ah — you and that man of mine seem to be gittin' pretty well acquainted," Big Jim muttered, surrendering himself completely.

Frazier suspected that Cantrell would hardly have said "that man of mine" had Lin been present. She decided to take toll for Lin.

"Yes," she smiled, "I am very fond of Lin."

Cantrell winced. "I hope he comes out of this inquest without any trouble," said he, managing to convey the insinuation that such might not be the case.

He was only paying her back in her own coin. He knew for a certainty that no one was going to be charged with killing Cèsar. It was Cantrell's turn to smile to himself now, for his shot struck home.

"Surely you don't mean that he will be accused? You know he had nothing to do with the boy's death!"

"I'd hate to think so, and I'm not sayin' anythin'. That's more than your father's doin'. It wouldn't be a bad idea to tell him to lay off," he finished. "Talk sometimes runs away with you."

"And sometimes it says more than one intends," she answered deeply, beginning to realize that he was only hoping to turn her against Lin.

Cantrell glanced at her and tried to read her unspoken thought. "What do you mean?" he was tempted to ask.

"Just that you are less loyal to him than he is to you. I expected to hear you defend him."

"Every man has got to look out for himself. That's my motto!"

"Evidently!"

Cantrell could have kicked himself for his foolish words.

"Well, no use us arguin'. The inquest will tell the story. Crocker is a great man for facts."

"I wish I shared your conviction," Frazier said plainly.

Cantrell shifted his eyes. "You surprise me," he declared. "Your father has turned things upside down to have the inquest held. I didn't oppose it just on that account. Maybe it will clear up things."

"Don't try to deceive me," Frazier answered pointedly. "As you well know this is only a farce staged to appease my father and the Basques! They are completely fooled. I congratulate you."

Cantrell was so exasperated that for the moment he forgot to dissemble his rage.

"Why — why — that's — why how can you say that?" he stammered. "That's dangerous talk. I warn you!"

"The truth is often dangerous," Frazier replied easily. She felt well repaid for the alarm he had given her a few minutes previous.

Cantrell was glad to see Angel drive into the yard. It gave him a convenient excuse for quitting the porch. But Frazier's caustic tongue and levelheadedness only made her more desirable. He had promised himself that she should belong to him, and he renewed that vow as he picked up his hat.

"To-morrow's Sunday," he announced, summoning a smile to his lips. "It's mighty pretty up in the peaks. Would you like to ride up there in the afternoon?"

94

Frazier shook her head regretfully for his benefit. "I'm sorry," she murmured, "but someone else has asked me already."

Cantrell turned away without another word, glaring at the world in general and hating Kincaid in particular.

"Serves him right," Frazier mused as she watched him go. No one had asked her to go riding, but she still hoped that Lin might.

CHAPTER
TEN

"Talk is Cheap"

A dozen hands were raised to help old Angel down from his buggy. His arrival silenced even the men who had so long opposed him.

He was almost an octogenarian, but those signs of age which manifest themselves in most men were strangely lacking in him. His hair was as thick as ever and almost as black. He was thin. His skin, the color of ripe old parchment, was so tightly drawn that not a wrinkle showed in his face.

As is usually the case, advancing years had only emphasized the strength of his features. It was a face to have delighted a Velasquez or a Murillo.

Time had left its marks on him, to be sure, but it had also left its caresses. The dignity of the man was unassailable. Even his enemies respected him — some without realizing it. Cantrell, for instance.

Life had made Angel Irosabal stern — too stern at times. His very pride had proven his weakness as well as his strength. Others before Irquieaga had questioned his wisdom and authority, but as Frazier Thane glanced from Angel to the burly Ramon, thick of neck and heavy jawed, she wondered how men could turn from the patriarch to follow the bully.

This was the first time the two men had met publicly in weeks. Irquieaga was not yet ready to measure forces with Angel, but, as has been previously stated, he had not dared to stay away to-day.

Frazier noticed his black look as all but the men with whom he had arrived deserted him and gathered about Angel. She also remarked how closely Wheeler and the other cattlemen regarded him. Most of them spoke to him as he approached the table at which the coroner sat.

"Been waitin' for you," Crocker informed him. "I want you to sit on the jury."

Angel nodded solemnly.

"Who are the other members?" he inquired. He made the question sound casual enough, but Crocker and Del Ryan exchanged a rather uneasy glance.

"Why — Bridger, Mr. Ryan, Thad Taylor and Jim Cantrell," Crocker answered, checking off the names on a sheet of paper that lay before him. It was not necessary for Crocker to refer to the written list; he knew well enough who was to serve. That he glanced at it was only to avoid meeting Angel's eyes — a bit of byplay, by the way, which better men than Crocker have used.

Cantrell nudged Bridger as the old Basque heard the names called off. Chris returned a knowing wink. No sign of chagrin or disappointment blossomed in Angel's face, however. He waited until Crocker had to look up.

"I am sorry, *Señor*," he announced patiently, "but you must excuse me."

"What do you mean?" Crocker exclaimed. "I want your people represented. I waited for you especially. I understood you wanted an inquest."

Angel took his time about answering.

"We do! Cèsar was my grandson. He had no enemies among his own people; no Basque killed him. I, for one, do not think it would be difficult to discover the guilty parties. But I am not innocent enough to believe that a jury composed of four cattlemen and one Basque will ever find out."

"You're taking the wrong idea," Del exclaimed. "We ain't trying the sheep question."

"No, you are not," Angel replied, still patient, "but Cèsar was killed because he was a herder."

"At least hear the evidence," Aaron urged. "I am sure Mr. Crocker did not intend any discrimation."

"Of course not," Nate exclaimed. Bridger and one or two others echoed this sentiment.

Angel smiled at them. He was not to be fooled.

"But I must refuse," said he. "I am an old man. When *Señor* Thane spoke to me of the inquest, I was interested but skeptical — my memory is long, remember — and I am even more skeptical now."

Cantrell muttered something angrily under his breath. Angel singled him out as a consequence.

"In the past, my people have been warned, even as you are warning us now. We have never warned you, but I warn you now! Cèsar was a good boy; he was very

98

dear to me. His death will not go unexplained, nor unpunished."

There was something in the old Basque's eyes that made Cantrell's blood run cold. What had he found out?

Aaron was more disappointed than Crocker at the turn things had taken. Nate, however, was angry as well as disappointed. Accordingly, he puffed out his cheeks like a grampus and glared defiantly.

"I can't see what all that's got to do with this inquest," he thundered. "I have ordered it in the name of the State of Nevada, and I'm going to hold it. You want this matter cleared up, you say. Well, we're here to do it. If you don't want to serve, I'll appoint someone else."

Angel bowed to him. "You will have to do that," said he. "I refuse to lend myself to a jury that will only whitewash the guilty parties in the hope that further investigation will not be necessary."

The Basques were silent as they heard him out, but an angry murmur ran through the ranks of the cattlemen.

"He wouldn't talk to me like that," Cantrell said threateningly.

Angel turned to him courteously. "Talk is very cheap, *Señor*," he declared with the blandest of smiles.

There was something more direct in this challenge than the words themselves implied. Cantrell felt it. He would have retorted violently had not Del silenced him with a look.

"Appoint someone else," the level-headed Wheeler called out.

"That's right; get this over with," another exclaimed.

Angel walked back to his buggy, a crowd following him. Aaron was tempted to speak to him further, but this cry for someone to take Angel's place held him chained where he stood beside Crocker, hoping he might be chosen.

But Nate had made one mistake to-day; he was in no mood to make another.

"All right, you take his place, Wheeler," he announced.

The jury was sworn in and the witnesses called. By this time the Basques were riding away. Irquieaga and his followers had left already. In another five minutes there was not a Basque in the yard.

The inquest did not take long. Lin, Flash and the Thanes were the only witnesses called. The jury retired to the porch for a few minutes. Followed then a word with Crocker. The verdict, "death by gunshot wounds administered by parties unknown" followed as a matter of course.

Justice? Why, it was hardly according to law.

There was an undercurrent to the affair that depressed Frazier so greatly that Lin had to ask twice before she consented to go riding with him the following afternoon.

Aaron shared his daughter's feeling.

"Irosabal should have stayed," he declared. "If Angel had been on the jury something might have come of it.

But he wouldn't listen to reason. He's getting so old he's childish."

"Do you really think so, Father? I thought he was magnificent," Frazier exclaimed feelingly.

Aaron looked at her, a little bit aghast that she should take sides against him.

"Frazier, don't forget you are only a girl. You don't understand these things."

"I wonder if it isn't you who do not understand, Father," she answered, refusing to give ground.

"Has it come to this that my own daughter criticizes me?" he exclaimed, bristling with indignation.

Frazier threw her arms around his neck and hugged him affectionately. "Don't be an old goose, Father," she implored. "I am not criticizing you, even though we do disagree now and then. I didn't like that man Crocker at all, and I was awfully glad to hear Mr. Irosabal say what he did."

"What have you got against Crocker?"

"Oh he was too friendly with Cantrell and his crowd. Why should Jim Cantrell have been on that jury? They found that boy on his range."

"So Kincaid claims," Aaron retorted sharply.

"And I believe him! Why is it no one suspects Cantrell? Perhaps they do and are afraid to say so."

Aaron held up a warning hand. "Don't you be the one to say it," he exclaimed. "Cantrell is a powerful man. It was some hot-headed, irresponsible cowpuncher who shot that boy."

"If you mean Lin, I think it's awfully unfair."

"Lin?" Aaron echoed. "You call him Lin already?"

"Well, Mr. Kincaid, then," Frazier replied. Her father was watching her closely and she blushed despite herself.

"I wouldn't get too interested in that young man," he said stiffly. "You must not forget that you are a Thane, Frazier."

"If all men show me equal respect the Thanes can rest in peace," she exclaimed frankly, hiding her impatience as best she could.

Since coming West she had found her father increasingly difficult to handle. She turned the conversation back to the inquest. She felt that he should not have urged it. Aaron thought otherwise.

"But, Father, we must think of ourselves. Don't let us be the buffer between the Basques and these cattlemen. Did you know the Lazy K cattle were raided last night?"

Aaron could not hide his surprise. "Why, no," he admitted. "Cantrell didn't mention it. Who told you? Kincaid, I presume."

Frazier nodded that he had.

Aaron was visibly relieved. "Funny nothing was said about this to-day," he muttered, at no pains to conceal his skepticism.

Frazier bit her lip. Once more Lin's veracity was being questioned. He seemed fated to be the subject of their conversation to-day. "Why do you always doubt him, Father?" she asked, her patience almost at an end.

"Because I can't believe that Cantrell would have met these Basques to-day and held his peace if he had been raided last night. It is not at all like the man to do that!"

"I fancy he would have said something had it not been for Mr. Ryan. They were so anxious to have the inquest a matter of record that Cantrell was forced to hold his tongue. Once, he almost said too much at it was. That nothing more was said may seem even stranger when I tell you that the men they suspect were present."

"Who?" Aaron gasped, a baffled look creeping into his eyes.

"That big man, Irquieaga, and his friends. Didn't you notice that they came heavily armed?"

Aaron laughed condescendingly now. This was going too far.

"You are letting your imagination run away with you, my child," he chided her. "Men often go armed. Don't ask me to believe that two such hot-heads as Cantrell and Irquieaga could have met here peaceably if what you are saying was true."

Was it possible that he would *not* understand? Frazier had seldom been so provoked with him.

"Father," she exclaimed, "do you remember that you called my attention to the sky over west last night? You thought there was a fire somewhere. Well, that fire was the Lazy K hay burning. It was a ruse to draw in the men Cantrell had riding his line. It worked successfully. As Angel Irosabal said, talk is cheap. Cantrell will have recourse to something more forceful than talk when he strikes back. I'm afraid he will not be any too careful where he hits."

Aaron had nothing to say to this. It had been a bad day generally for him and he sulked now as he realized that he had blundered a second time.

"Lin says there will be reprisals," Frazier added unwittingly.

"Lin! Lin!" old Aaron grumbled as he pushed back his chair and got to his feet. "I'll ride up there this afternoon and see for myself what happened."

Frazier ran after him. "Don't go away angry, Father," she pleaded.

Aaron melted rather than see tears in her eyes. "Who is angry?" he demanded. "Run along, now, I'll be back early."

Frazier watched him ride away. He seemed less than a match for a lean, hard-riding man like Cantrell. And yet at that very moment Big Jim was worried on his own account.

Bridger had stopped for a bite to eat before going on to Quinn River. They had discussed the inquest. Cantrell was finally tempted to ask Chris if he thought Angel had found out anything.

"Jes' talk, I take it," said Bridger.

The answer failed to satisfy Cantrell. He had seen something in the old Basque's eyes that had thoroughly alarmed him.

"Why did he address himself to me, then?" he demanded.

Bridger laughed coldly. "You ask that?" he inquired. "You ought to know why, Jim."

Cantrell chose not to be offended by this directness.

"Say what you will, he wasn't bluffin'. I don't think he knows anythin' — but he aims to, and that'll get him somewhere eventually."

They smoked in silence for some time. Cantrell could not throw off his moodiness.

"I never saw your face so long," Chris declared. "Angel must have put the fear of God into you. Or is it Del who's worryin' you?"

Cantrell was too absorbed with his own thoughts to care much what Bridger said. Unconsciously his brooding began to affect Chris.

"What's on your mind?" the latter insisted at last.

Minutes passed before Cantrell replied. Wheeler's attitude worried him. Del had been equally disturbing. Most significant of all, however, was Angel's defiance. Cantrell was almost ready to admit that he had made a mistake, but that admission could be made only to himself, for by nature, he was suspicious of all men, even Bridger.

The thought that was uppermost in his mind finally took definite shape and he brought his chair down on all fours as a signal that he had reached a decision.

"Just this," he announced, "somethin's got to be done about that boy Cèsar. Somebody has got to produce the guilty parties. I reckon I can do that."

"So-o-o!" Bridger exclaimed. "You mean —"

"You know who I mean!" Cantrell cut him off. "No need of mentionin' names. You keep out of this, Chris; I'll handle it by myself."

"I'd go slow, Jim. You ain't monkeyin' with kids," Bridger warned. He had made some observations of his own to-day.

"I'll go slow enough. Don't you worry about that," Cantrell assured him. "I'll frame 'em first and accuse 'em afterwards!"

Bridger tried to draw him out, but at the end of half an hour he gave up and went on home. Left to himself, Cantrell lost no time in putting his plans into execution.

CHAPTER
ELEVEN

Birds of a Feather

At breakfast the following morning, Cantrell announced that he was leaving for the Owyhee country to buy horses. So, shortly after breakfast, while Lin was shaving himself in preparation for the afternoon with Frazier, Cantrell rode off.

The Owyhee Basin lies a hundred miles due east from Paradise Valley. Once there, Cantrell's way would be to the south and the little town of Tuscarora.

Back in the late 80's when the bonanza days were fast drawing to a close and Fair, Mackay and Flood had succeeded in ripping a fortune out of the Comstock, Tuscarora had had its day. Men of all kinds and many races had tried for fortune there. And Tuscarora had blazed brightly. Stamp mills had been erected. The nearest railroad was fifty miles away. Ore had to be reduced on the spot to make it profitable.

Twenty-mule teams took out the bullion. Picturesque characters walked the streets, and, inevitably, those painted ladies of the evening, those barometers of a mining town's prosperity who ever are the first to come and the first to leave.

107

It was wild, wide open and strictly hard cash. Some there were who thought it would last forever. Suddenly it was gone.

The machinery in the mills was not worth the cost of taking out. Houses could not be packed on a wagon and carted off. And as Cantrell caught his first glimpse of the empty town he found it little changed, although he had not laid eyes on it in four years. But then, in that altitude, neither four years nor many times four years would work any great changes in that silent city.

Cantrell was no stranger here. The man he sought was one of the dozen or more who still lingered there, some because they were too poor to leave, others because it was a safe retreat, and it was the latter reason that interested the individual whom Cantrell had come to see.

Big Jim entered the Chinese quarter at the base of the hill and turned his horse up the quiet length of the once bustling main street. He passed the once ornate emporium where Denver Joe had held forth, catering to the thirsty. The sunlight filtered in crazily through its broken windows.

Just across the street stood the derelict Silver State Saloon and Dance Hall, once the pride of Tuscarora, but only a haunted sepulchre to-day.

At the four corners there were still signs of life — a stable, a general-store and a saloon.

The sun was shining warmly, but Big Jim shook himself to throw off the chill which these old scenes gave him and urged his horse on. He drew up at the corner before the old Gem. The long hitching-rack was deserted. Through the uncurtained windows of the saloon he perceived that no one leaned against the long bar at which it once had been a privilege to stand and spend.

As Cantrell entered, the proprietor emerged from the shadows in back of the bar. Cantrell nodded curtly.

"Diamond Jim!" the man exclaimed. "Why, I wouldn't a known you, Jim, if visitors wasn't so scarce that we look twice at everyone who comes."

He would have shaken hands, but Cantrell was less cordial. "Let's have a drink," said he.

"I guess you find things changed a little, Jim. I heard you was down in Californy."

"Yes? You can hear most anythin' these days."

Cantrell came no nearer to enlightening him, and the man did not press the question.

"Some of the boys are working over the old tailings and taking out a day's pay," he rumbled on. "Tuscarora ain't so dead as she looks."

Cantrell was not interested.

"Where'll I find Joe Dolores?" he asked.

The man smiled inscrutably. Without knowing what business brought Cantrell there he was able to surmise the nature of it now. Dolores had been Diamond Jim's man Friday in the old days when there had been suckers to trim and the case ace was often necessary. Scenting a profit to himself, he became evasive.

"Why, he's in the Basin somewhere," said he.

"But I'm not goin' to spend a week lookin' for him," Cantrell exclaimed impatiently. "Joe wrote me you could tell me where to find him."

Cantrell was lying. The man's smile broadened.

"Joe is putting on airs, writing letters and all that," he laughed. He knew Joe could not write his own name. "You might leave word here for him, Jim," he went on. "Dolores drops in once in a while."

He knew where Joe was. In fact, he was one of the Mexican's paid retainers. But he was not giving away information that could be sold. If Cantrell wanted to see Joe, he stood ready to pilot him to the Mexican's roost in the deep cañon of Columbia Creek.

By now Cantrell understood him perfectly.

"You're pretty cagey, Billy," he said condescendingly. "I reckon you could show me the way." He paid for the drinks and rolled a twenty-dollar gold piece across the bar to the man. "You got a horse?"

The man nodded as he pocketed the coin.

"Well, let's ride," Cantrell suggested. "This place gives me the willies."

The camp on Columbia Creek just suited Dolores. The country was wild and broken. No one ventured there by design and few by accident.

There are men who gravitate naturally to the fringe of things. Dolores was one. He had dealt faro, played capper, traded in contraband, and now for two years men had hinted that he ran an iron on other folks' stock.

So far, the broken-down place on Columbia Creek, with its shack and barn and corral, had proved a safe retreat. It was dirty and uncomfortable; but that mattered little to Dolores and his men.

110

The cañon could be entered only from below, so, whenever the corral held any evidence that would have turnd rumor to fact, which was very seldom, they had but to post a man at the mouth of the cañon to be warned in time and over the hills and the Idaho line long before a blow could be struck.

Dolores was interested only in horses; they could be moved swiftly, and usually there was only the brand on the stifle to contend with.

But the real secret of Dolores' success was the natural corral he had found in that blistered section of the Basin proper, known as the Lava Beds. No cowboy thought of looking in the Lava Beds for strays, nor did any miner dream of finding mineral in their depths. It was a place to avoid.

And yet Dolores had found a spring there. Food he carried in. To the north, lay Idaho, his best market. When the time seemed propitious, he moved his stuff. It was profitable, as safe as such ventures can be, and entirely to his liking.

Cantrell's first glimpse of the nest on Columbia Creek assured him that he had not come on a fool's errand. Dolores greeted him cordially; they had understood each other very well in the old days. Strangely enough they did not reminisce. The memories of such men are best forgotten. Swarthy Dolores waited for Cantrell to state his mission.

"I want to buy some horses, Joe," Cantrell told him at last. "Have you got some good ones?"

"Yes, I half planty good wan, Jeem," Dolores smiled, his white teeth gleaming.

"Got 'em here, Joe?"

"You see any, Jeem?" the Mexican asked with a knowing grin. "Those nags in the corral ees just some stuff belongs to the boys. They may be starched a leetla bit in the laigs, but they know how to look a sheriff right in the eye, Jeem."

They laughed together at this jest.

"I'm not goin' to ask you where you've got 'em," Cantrell continued. "I want 'em young and likely lookin'; horses that you might think a man would travel three or four days to pick up. You understand?"

Dolores nodded, wondering why Cantrell was so willing to trust him. The Diamond Jim he knew had had the reputation of driving a hard bargain always.

"How much you goin' to charge me?" Cantrell demanded.

Dolores threw up his hands. "Wait," he said. "Where you goin' to tak' those horse, Jeem?"

"Why — why, over in the Little Humboldt country. I'll send over after 'em the end of this week or the first of next."

Dolores shook his head now and shifted his legs to a more comfortable position. "These horse of mine ain't safe west of the Owyhee," he volunteered. "I don' want mak' no trouble for you, Jeem. Eef your men start through that country maybe somewan ask where they get those horse. *Por Dios*, I not lak to half them say from Joe Dolores."

"So that's where the stuff came from originally, eh, between the Owyhee and the county line? That suits me fine! Why should my men know anythin' about you? We can fix that up!"

"Maybe so! But I tall you, those men get nabbed sure."

Cantrell caught his eye and held it. "Maybe that's what I've got on my mind," he muttered.

Now Dolores understood him better.

Cantrell was not averse to showing his hand. Too much depended on Dolores for him to leave anything to chance.

It was not difficult for Joe to follow him as he unfolded his plans. In fact it was the sort of trickery he was best fitted to understand.

"Don't think I'm sendin' you a pair of kids," Cantrell warned him.

"I don't know these men, eh?"

"You don't know one of 'em, McCarroll. The other one used to work in the Basin. His name's Lin Kincaid — a big tall fellow."

Dolores shook his head. "I don't know heem. Maybe he knows me, though."

"You won't appear in this deal, Joe. All I want you to do is boss the job. Now don't underestimate my men. If they get suspicious they won't touch those horses. Look out for the tall one; he's no fool."

"You leave that to me, Jeem," Dolores assured Cantrell. "I mak' no meestak' for my own sake."

"I hope not. Now, Joe, I want you to tell me just where this string of horses came from. I'll see that they go back that very way. Trouble will be certain to catch up with 'em, then!"

Dolores obliged. The price was soon arranged.

"If this thing goes through, there'll be somethin' extra in it for you," Cantrell told him. "I'll see to that!"

Dolores wanted to know where he was to turn over the stolen horses, even suggesting that he would risk bringing them to Columbia Creek. "Don't do that!" Cantrell swore. "They'd be wise in a minute. Why, you've only got to get a flash at this place to know it's a hide-out."

"I guess eet ain't so swell," Dolores grumbled.

"Now don't get sore!" Big Jim threw in hurriedly. "You got me wrong, Joe."

"Well, I don't tak' them to my corral, no matter what you pay," he said flatly.

"Of course not! Shake up somethin' to eat; I'll figure this thing out to a T."

After they had eaten, Cantrell lost no time in getting back to business. "All that range east of the South Fork between the Bull Run Mountains and the Tuscaroras still belongs to the Double Square, doesn't it?"

Dolores answered that it did.

"I didn't see much stuff there when I came through yesterday. They ain't likely to have many men there this time of the year."

"Not many," Dolores agreed.

"Well, could you get your string moved over near the South Fork without bein' seen?"

Dolores shrugged his shoulders. Probably he could. How could one be certain?

"Supposin' you could, do you think you could hold them there on the Double Square range for half a day? You could move out if you had to."

114

Dolores admitted that this might be done.

"All right! Now what about the brands? How are they marked?"

"I have not touch them yet."

"That's good! I was afraid you mighta put your own brand on 'em. I don't want any registered brand to figure in this."

"I guess I don't want any either." Dolores smiled knowingly.

"Of course not! You've got a week to get ready in. You used to be a wonder with an iron. Can you get these brands doctored up in that time? I don't want 'em to look sore."

"Don't worry 'bout that. How you want 'em marked?"

"Whatever will be easiest."

Dolores pondered over the matter for several minutes and got out a pencil and covered a soiled envelope with strange marks.

"I can make over most anytheeng to a S B Bar brand. You've got to do eet weeth a pointing iron and a razor; not by over-branding."

"Is it registered?"

"I look eet up now."

He got out a badly-thumbed copy of the state record of registered brands.

"No one using eet," he announced. "I mak' sure I peeck out for you only those brands I can work over easy, Jeem."

"That seems to be all right," Cantrell mused aloud. "You do that! Get your horses down near those hard-pan flats east of the South Fork next Monday afternoon. Post a man on the river at the crossin'. Have him there all day, and be sure he knows where the horses are. He'll meet my men and tell them where to find the stuff. Have him make it appear that he's ridin' for the Double Square. They still use Mexican *vaqueros*, don't they?"

"Yeh! Plentee."

"Now! You see, that means my men will git in and away without askin' any questions of the wrong people. You keep out of sight, Joe. Leave just one man to turn over the horses. He's supposed to be workin' for this S B Bar brand that's leasin' that range. That'll be about all you'll have to do. I'll tell you again, so you'll not slip up."

A second telling was not necessary, but Cantrell insisted on it.

"That's almost too easy, Jeem," Dolores nodded. "Eef those horse ees recognized, those men of your have damn hard time proving they deedn't change those brands."

"Exactly! It's mighty bad to be caught with stolen horses in your possession, no matter how you come by 'em. When they're wearin' an unregistered brand it's even worse. If they try to prove that they're actin' on orders from me, they won't help themselves. How will they be able to prove where the stuff was turned over to 'em? It won't take long to find out that no one ever heard of any S B Bar brand in the Basin, and old Lief Forgetsen will tell 'em he never leased any range to any

116

such brand or to any such person as Kincaid and McCarroll will claim they did business with."

"Eet may come back to you, Jeem," Dolores suggested skeptically. "What you say then?"

Cantrell laughed loudly. "I'm ready for that! I ain't overlooked it. When I get home I'll pack Kincaid and McCarroll off in a hurry. They'll leave with the understandin' that they're to meet this S B Bar man that they believe is workin' for some small leaser. Soon as they're out of sight I'll see that it gets around that I've sent 'em over here to bring back some stuff I've bought of the *Double Square* — and to make that good, I'm goin' to stop at Forgetsen's to-day and pay him for a dozen horses and tell him my boys will be over next Monday to get 'em."

Dolores inhaled his cigarette with keen relish and gazed at Cantrell in open admiration.

"If they try to pull any S B Bar story on me, I'll just laugh at 'em. It will be my word against theirs — and I'll have witnesses to prove that the horses they came to get were Double Square horses!"

"*Por Dios!*" Dolores blasphemed. "You always was ver' clever, Jeem!

CHAPTER
TWELVE

"Dead to Rights!"

In due course the stolen horses were turned over to Lin and Flash as Cantrell had planned. They were suspicious — but not of the horses. Lin felt that the trip to the Basin was only a ruse to get Flash and him out of the way for a few days. In the time that he had worked for Cantrell the Lazy K had never had less need of more horses. Then, too, it seemed strange that with trouble certain to come Cantrell should find it advisable to weaken his own hand by sending them away for a week.

Lin knew that something was afoot — something desperate, too — and where Cantrell was concerned that might mean anything. During the long trip to the Basin, he and Flash discussed little else than what was likely to transpire in their absence.

Naturally, Kincaid worried about Frazier. He could not believe that Cantrell would have maneuvered to get them out of the way were he contemplating nothing more than an attack on some Basque's flock to avenge the raid on the Lazy K.

So Cantrell succeeded easier than he had thought to, and once the string of stolen horses had been turned

118

over to their charge, Kincaid and McCarroll lost no time in starting west.

They had previously decided to travel day and night until they reached the ranch. It was still early evening when they got back to the South Fork. The aroma of boiling coffee assailed their nostrils as they neared the crossing. A few moments later they were hailed from the opposite side of the stream.

"Howdy!" a man called, standing over his fire. His horse was picketed nearby and it was evident he intended camping there the night.

They waved him a greeting. The man was a stranger; but that made little difference. They were hungry, and that is usually enough to win an invitation to eat.

"Just in time," Flash chuckled as they forded the stream.

Lin thought that the welcome he had seen in the stranger's eyes began to dim. He was scrutinizing their horses now and trying to pretend that he wasn't.

Lin and Flash got out of their saddles and stretched their legs as the horses drank. McCarroll's hint that they wouldn't refuse a bite to eat went unanswered, even though the man beside the fire could see that they carried only their blankets.

"Have a cigarette?" Flash asked, eyeing the coffee-pot.

"Don't smoke," the man answered and then, to their surprise, began to gather up his roll.

"We ain't drivin' you out?" Flash inquired caustically.

"No. Suppose you're goin' west?"

Somehow the question sounded more important just then than the words themselves signify.

Lin felt it.

"That's usually the idea in crossin' the South Fork," he drawled pointedly.

The stranger did not reply, but wiped out his frying-pan and poured out the contents of his coffee-pot. He began to saddle up then.

"You don't mind leavin' us the fire do yuh?" Flash inquired with contempt.

"No, help yourselves," the man answered.

He was gone presently. Lin and Flash looked at each other with a puzzled frown.

"What scared him so?" Lin asked.

"Scared?"

"You bet he was scared."

"Must be somethin' wrong with us," Flash muttered, "throwin' that coffee —"

"Wasn't us he was lookin' at," Lin interrupted. His tone was so serious that Flash pulled himself up sharply. "I'd a swore he recognized these broncs — recognized them real personal, too."

"My God, you mean there's somethin' wrong with 'em?"

For answer Lin reached out and ran his hand over the brand on the horse nearest him. The mare trembled, and when he pinched the hide near the stifle-joint, the animal squealed.

Lin shook his head gravely.

"Mighty tender!" Flash exclaimed.

120

"Sure is!" Lin repeated the experiment on another horse. "Those brands look all right if you don't examine them too closely," he muttered. "I swear they ain't a week old."

"Holy Moses! You mean Cantrell has handed us a stacked deck? We should have tumbled when he said we wouldn't need a bill of sale. Turned 'em over to us out in the open! No witnesses — Nothin'! Like as not these horses belong around here. Us tryin' to git through at night won't look good to anyone. What are we goin' to do, Lin?"

"Keep our heads, for one thing. Cantrell can have only one reason for wantin' to discredit us. You know what that is. If we get turned up as a pair of horse thieves, he'll start in to prove that we're killers as well."

"But we can prove that he sent us over here to get these broncs."

"Can we?" Lin asked skeptically. "It'll be his word against ours, and he's got the drag, not us. You stay here a minute, Flash. I'm goin' to trail that *hombre* a ways."

The ground swelled away to low hills just west of the South Fork, so in a few minutes Lin passed from sight. He was back in less than half an hour.

"He's fannin' it for all he's worth, straight for the Circle D outfit headquarters on Chino Creek," Lin reported. "We're goin' to travel *fast*, Flash. We may be foolin' ourselves, but I don't aim to stay here and find out. Let's go!"

Twilight deepened to night as they rode. It slackened their pace.

"The moon will be up early to-night," Flash called out.

"That won't help us any," Lin replied curtly. "Haze 'em along!"

The wind began to blow. The remuda moved faster. Later, when they reached Chino Creek, they churned the water to silver spray that flashed from their hoofs as they dashed across the stream. It was dark in the creek bottom. Soon they were in the open again. It was lighter now.

"There comes your damned moon," Lin muttered.

"And here comes our friends!" Flash flung back at him.

Half a mile off a flying cavalcade bore down on them.

"Pull up!" Lin ordered. "We're in for it. Don't lie to these men, Flash. They won't believe us, but we've got to stick to the truth."

McCarroll cursed Cantrell bitterly. "He'll pay for this!" he swore.

"I reckon he will," Lin answered. "Here they are!"

"Throw up yore hands!" a voice barked. "Climb!"

There was nothing to do but oblige. A dozen men surrounded them. The man who had left the South Fork so hurriedly was among those present.

"Hand over yore guns," a wizened little man commanded. "Some of you boys tie 'em up."

"Well, I *do* be damned!" exclaimed the one who came forward to truss up Kincaid. "Lin Kincaid! I never thought you'd git down to runnin' horses, Lin."

Lin recognized the man.

"Tim Jafferay," he drawled.

The little man looked from one to the other. "You two acquainted?" he asked Jafferay.

"Used to work together for the Bar Cross," said Tim. "His name's Lin Kincaid."

"Humph!" the little man muttered noncommittally.

"Never heard a word ag'in him, either," Tim threw in for good measure.

"Humph!" the little man exclaimed again. "Tie him up anyhow." He moved off to examine the horses. Those who had come with him had already identified them, as their sullen glances at Kincaid and McCarroll eloquently testified.

"This roan is yours, Hunter," someone said to the little man. "They ought to have their necks stretched, the damned thieves!"

"Sure had," Hunter replied as he examined the horse.

He came back to Kincaid presently.

"I reckon we got you fellers about dead to rights," said he. "If you make a move to get away it will be yore last one."

"You goin' to convict us without givin' us a chance to prove ourselves innocent?" Lin asked easily.

"You'll git yore chance before a judge maybe," Hunter snapped. "We been missin' horses too long to be talked out of anythin' to-night."

"Well, you'll continue to miss them if you think you've got the right parties in us. We're from the Humboldt country, workin' for the Lazy K outfit. We were sent over here to get these broncs. They were turned over to us this afternoon."

"Who turned 'em over to you?"

Lin paused for a moment. He didn't know the man's name.

"An S B Bar man," he said a little lamely.

"Who's the S B Bar?" some one demanded. "Never heard of the brand!"

"Where's their range?" Hunter demanded.

"Why, they're leasin' from the Double Square," Lin replied.

This caused derisive laughter from all.

"They are, eh? Say, I was talkin' to Forgetsen yesterday. He's lost stuff too. He ain't leased an acre to anyone. Your story don't hold water."

"Leasin' from Forgetsen," a burly individual muttered sarcastically. The rest took it up.

"What's the sense of wastin' time talkin' to him?" another wanted to know.

"That's what I say!" exclaimed the man Lin and Flash had met at the South Fork crossing.

Flash glared angrily at him. Lin pretended not to be ruffled.

"Do you think we would have come back this way with stuff that belonged here?" he asked.

"It's night," Hunter answered; "you might have got through. We weren't lookin' for you here."

"It's night, all right," Lin persisted, "but we got an inklin' of trouble when your friend there left us at the crossin'. We could have turned back or dropped this

124

string and saved ourselves. A horse-thief ain't much good to himself in jail."

"You should have given that some thought quite a time back," the little man informed him acidly. "Who did you say you was workin' for?"

"Cantrell — Jim Cantrell," Lin informed him.

"Humph!" Hunter exclaimed once more. "I ain't sure to positive, but it seems to me that's the name of the man Forgetsen mentioned yesterday. He just happened to say he'd sold a little bunch of horses."

A deep understanding dawned in Kincaid's eyes. He and Flash exchanged a furtive glance. Any doubt that Cantrell had deliberately and craftily plotted against them was gone on the instant.

"Sure, they're lyin'; anything to stall us off," the man from the river grumbled.

Nevertheless, Kincaid managed to smile confidently.

"I reckon we'll be cleared easy enough," he drawled. "It won't take the sheriff long to get in touch with Cantrell."

"That's right," Flash supplemented, taking his cue from Lin, "this little mix-up will be ironed out to-morrow. We got the horses we was sent to git."

"I hope so, for your sake, Lin," Tim Jafferay said.

No one else echoed his interest or optimism.

"We'll take 'em over to my place," Hunter announced after consulting one or two others. "It'll be mornin' before the sheriff can get up here. We can talk this thing over. If you're ready, we'll move."

"Wouldn't be a bad idea for a few of us to take a swing east of the South Fork; these two ain't all of the gang we're after."

This was agreed to promptly. The two parties separated, one moving to the east and the other north to the Circle D.

Lin and Flash managed to exchange a guarded word as they rode along. "You know what Cantrell will say when it's put up to him," McCarroll murmured.

"Certainly! Like as not he's already spread the report that he sent us to Forgetsen's. You follow my lead, Flash. Don't seem to take this seriously; maybe they'll untie our hands if they see we ain't got no idea of makin' a break."

When the posse reached the Circle D, the two prisoners were placed in an unused cook-shed. It was bare, save for a table and an old bench. There was but one window, and it was securely fastened.

Jafferay and another man were left to stand guard over them. "Shall we untie them?" Jafferay asked.

Hunter hesitated over his answer a moment. "Yes, I guess they ain't foolish enough to try to get away," he said.

The others turned their horses into the corral and moved over near the barn. They soon had a fire going. Lin could see them squatting around it on the ground.

"Say, Tim, is there any chance of gettin' a bite to eat and a little water?" Lin inquired. "We ain't tasted anythin' since mornin."

"I'll ask the boss," Jafferay answered.

He called Hunter over and made the request known to him.

"I'll have somethin' sent down from the house," he told them.

Half an hour later one of Hunter's Piute servants arrived with a jug of water and basket of food. Lin chatted easily with Tim as he and Flash ate.

"Still as good a story-teller as you used to be at the Bar Cross?" Tim inquired. "That's goin' to be a long time ago, Lin."

Lin was only too willing to oblige. Flash got his mouth-organ and played and sang. Tim and the other man sat on the doorstep. Every once in a while an inquisitive eye was turned on them from the group seated around the fire.

"Hope you get out of this as easy as you think," said Tim.

"Don't worry; we'll get out," Lin assured him. "Give me another cigarette."

Tim had no more.

"I'll get some," the man seated beside Tim offered. He was halfway to the fire when Lin got up to get another drink. Flash was watching him closely.

"I hate to do this, Tim, but I reckon it's necessary," said Kincaid.

Tim looked up, not understanding, just as Lin hurled the jug at him. Jafferay stretched his length on the floor.

Kincaid grabbed his guns and handed one to Flash.

"*Sing!*" Lin commanded. He retrieved the jug. "We're goin' now, Flash! Our horses are in the corral, still saddled. If we get away, we'll split. I'll head west;

you go east. That ought to help our chances. You know where my old cabin is at the mine on Emigrant Creek. Look for me there if you have luck. Now sing — loud as you can!"

McCarroll wiped his brow. For the moment song was beyond him.

"Give 'em 'Windy Bill'!" Kincaid urged. And then, as Flash bawled his song, Lin hurled the jug through the window. It carried away the glass and most of the sash. "Come on!" he cried, "they'll be here in half a minute!"

The corral was in back of the cook-shed. They scaled the fence without coming into the light from the fire, but they wasted precious seconds in finding their horses.

The men were calling excitedly to one another. Five or six ran to the cook-shed.

"They're gone!" one shouted. Lin recognized Hunter's voice.

"Busted out the window!" another cried. "Jafferay's knocked out cold!"

Instinctively they ran to the corral now. Lin had the gate open.

"So long, Flash!" he cried as he drove Piñon straight for the oncoming men. They fell back before the madly driven horse. To give them further pause, Kincaid emptied his gun.

"Shoot! *Shoot!* you fools! What ails you?" Hunter screamed, and rushing up began firing wildly at the fleeing pair.

Before they could saddle their horses, Kincaid and McCarroll were half a mile away.

CHAPTER
THIRTEEN

Cantrell Declares Himself

Lin had left without saying good-bye to Frazier. It was Cantrell, stopping for a word, as had become his habit, who informed her that he had sent Kincaid to the Basin to bring back some horses he had bought from Lief Forgetsen. He had been careful to mention the name several times.

In answer to her question as to when Lin would be back, Big Jim had told her that he expected him by the middle of the following week. But Friday had come again without bringing a glimpse of Lin.

He was often in her thoughts. In truth, she had taken to comparing him with certain young men she knew back in Great Barrington. Unquestionably they would have thought him strange, and smiled behind his back at his rather quaint manner of speech. On the other hand, Lin would have felt quite the same way about them had they suddenly been set down on the range. For all the observations to the contrary, the East and the West were not yet one.

The list of those applying for grazing permits in the Reserve was to be published this day, and her father had gone to town in regard to it. A dozen and more times since he had left she had come to the door to gaze at the winding ribbon of dust that passed for a road, unconsciously looking for Kincaid. In mid-afternoon she was rewarded by seeing someone approaching from the west, and she leaped to the conclusion that it was Lin.

Some minutes before the rider turned into the yard she realized that it was Cantrell who was calling. It was difficult for her to hide her disappointment.

She noticed that Big Jim was better dressed than usual to-day. He smiled warmly. He was very confident of himself this afternoon.

Frazier's first thought was that he had come about the permits. There was something so sinister about the man that his presence always filled her with vague alarm.

"Why, you're as pritty as a picture to-day," he beamed as he flung himself into a chair beside her. "Every time I come here," he went on, "I realize more and more that a man shouldn't go on livin' alone like I been."

Frazier had a premonition of what was coming now, for Cantrell had embarked on this subject before. He pursued it again to-day.

"I suppose you have come to say something to Father about the grazing permits," Frazier exclaimed, hoping to turn the conversation from herself. "Father has gone to town."

Cantrell had hitched his chair a little nearer hers.

"I didn't come to see your father to-day," he murmured amorously.

Frazier did not fail to understand him.

"No? You've got news about Mr. Kincaid, then!" she exclaimed with malice aforethought.

Cantrell's head went up a little and his mouth lost its grin. "I didn't come to talk about my men, either," said he.

"Aren't they back?"

"Not yet. They should have been home day before yesterday."

"Nothing could have happened to them?" Frazier asked with real concern.

Cantrell felt that he could afford to speak generously of them. The fact that they were already two days overdue was the best proof in the world that they had been caught in the trap he had set for them.

"They know their business," he told her. "I reckon they'll turn up to-morrow. But as I was sayin' — I didn't come here to discuss Kincaid. He's a good enough bronc peeler; but that let's him out."

"I've heard other men speak more favorably of him," Frazier replied with a pretty toss of her head.

"Come now! we're not goin' to quarrel about Kincaid to-day," Cantrell proclaimed with bland assurance, "even though I hate to see you interested at all in a man that's in the habit of driftin' around from one job to another and who hasn't got a cent to his name, outside his wages. You're the type of woman that needs and oughta have pretty things. A cowpuncher can't give 'em to you."

"You take too much for granted, Mr. Cantrell," Frazier exclaimed as she drew back. "There is no thought of marriage in my mind."

"There is in mine!" Big Jim declared. He caught her hands and refused to release them. He knew that she belongd to a world far removed from his. But that made her even more desirable to him. The ways of respectability had never been his; and this from choice; but there were times, times when he was prosperous, that that which is the fruit of respectability and honor appealed strongly to him.

Cantrell was not deceiving himself into believing that she cared for him. His next words proved how he felt.

"I haven't the language I'd like to have to say what I'm goin' to say, Miss Frazier, but I've got the dollars to make up for it. I want you to be my wife. The moment I first laid eyes on you I knew you was the woman for me."

"Please, no, Mr. Cantrell!" Frazier cried as she struggled to free her hands. "Certainly I've given you no reason to believe that I care for you."

"I'm not askin' that," he exclaimed passionately. "Marry me and I'll see that you father don't lose out. You owe somethin' to him."

"But not what you suggest," Frazier gasped. "Please let me go! I never could marry you."

The wind brushed a strand of her hair across his cheek. Cantrell winced in the sheer ecstasy of his flaming desire. He drew her to him and lifted her face to his.

"No! *No!*" Frazier screamed.

"I *will* kiss you!" Cantrell muttered thickly. "You drive me mad!"

132

Fight him as she would he drew her face up until his lips hovered greedily over hers. What good to cry out for help? Her father was away; Esteban, the herder, miles off. If Cantrell was to be stopped, she must accomplish it herself.

Something was boring into her side as he strained her to him. It was Cantrell's gun.

Big Jim felt her go limp in his arms. He released her hands and covered her lips with his mad kisses. Suddenly she straightened.

"Get back!" she ordered. "I've got your gun. I'll shoot in another second."

The expression on Cantrell's face slowly changed. "By God, I believe you would at that," said he.

"What a beast you are," Frazier murmured contemptuously as he backed away. "I would kill myself sooner than marry you," she cried, and her words bit like a lash.

"I don't suppose I'm good enough for you," Cantrell spat out viciously. "You'll come to your senses soon enough. I tell you now that you're goin' to belong to me before we're through, whether you marry me or not."

Frazier's lips were white.

"Go!" she cried, "before I shoot you as you deserve!"

"Too bad your friend Kincaid ain't here to protect you," Cantrell laughed evily.

"I daresay he *would* find a way to protect me," she replied bravely.

"Well, don't you count too much on Kincaid. You may never see him again."

There was an undertone of meaning here that was unescapable.

"I fancy there are reasons why you would be glad to see him out of the way," Frazier taunted him, "reasons not connected with me. Have you plotted against him, too?"

Cantrell was without information regarding Kincaid and McCarroll. Had it been in his possession he would have asked for no better opportunity than this to deliver the news to her. Instead, he had to resort to evasion, and he did it lamely.

"You don't know cowpunchers!" he laughed. "It's here to-day and gone to-morrow with them. Why should they be two or three days late on a little trip to the Owyhee Basin? I know they've got a string of horses in their possession that belong to me. I'm doin' the worryin', not you!"

"And yet you were full of excuses for them when you came," she observed pointedly.

"Well, if it will make you feel any better, I don't mind tellin' you that if they don't show up to-morrow, I aim to find out where they are. And before I leave I want to promise you that if your father tries to use the permit he's in town to git to-day, he'll regret it. No Basque is goin' to run sheep into the Reserve, and that includes your father now. You've been warned a plenty. This is the last one you'll have. It's time for you folks to git out!"

Frazier did not leave the porch until he was out of sight. Weak and trembling she went into the house then and scrubbed herself as she had never done before.

134

She did not doubt that trouble would ride hard at their heels. It was against her wishes that her father had espoused the cause of the Basques in the slaying of Cèsar. Until to-day she had believed that they might remain neutral. That hope was gone forever.

She thought of old Angel and then of Cantrell, and took courage. She recalled how calmly and with what dignity the old Basque had faced his enemies. He had revealed himself as fully that day as Cantrell had this afternoon.

If left free to choose between them, who, she wondered, would have taken Cantrell? Surely if the men who stood with him were cut at all to his pattern she and her father were not to be pitied that events had definitely arrayed them with the Basques.

Lin's absence was difficult to explain. She dismissed Cantrell's insinuations. And yet the man knew more than he had said. She was certain of that; but she refused to believe that Lin was in trouble. Without knowing the country, she was sensible enough to realize that many things can happen on a trip of two hundred miles to delay a man several days.

Frazier knew if she ever repeated a word of what had occurred to-day to Kincaid that his days as a Lazy K man would end abruptly. Just how she could refuse to acquaint him with Cantrell's insinuations became something of a problem, and yet if she did he would undoubtedly leave the Humboldt country forever.

Old Aaron returned from town with his prized permit as she sat trying to solve the riddle that confronted her. He was in the best of spirits.

"Everything is all right now," he beamed. "We can send the flock in on the first of the month. Any number of Basques applied. The town was full of cattlemen. They put on a long face as they heard the names called out. Little good that will do them. Cantrell's foreman was there. I didn't see Cantrell himself."

Frazier could not bring herself to tell him what had occurred in his absence, other than that Cantrell had dropped in for a few minutes.

"He seems to be spending considerable time here," her father exclaimed questioningly.

"I guess we will see less of him from now on," Frazier replied deeply as she began preparations for supper.

Something in her tone caused Aaron to glance sharply at her. "What makes you say that?" he asked.

"Oh, nothing, Father. He didn't get the encouragement he expected, that's all."

"So that's what has been bringing him here," Aaron nodded weightily. "I declare! Why didn't he address himself to me first?"

"I'm afraid that isn't done out here," Frazier smiled wearily.

Aaron could get no more out of her and finally repaired to the porch to peruse his newspapers. He was back almost instantly with Cantrell's gun in his hand. Frazier's face fell at sight of it. "How stupid of me to forget it," she thought.

"Whose is this?" he demanded sternly.

"Why, why Mr. Cantrell left it here, I presume," she hurried to say. "You must return it to him to-morrow."

"That's strange," old Aaron snorted with fine contempt. "Never heard of a man leaving his gun behind, especially if he's as fond of one as Cantrell. You *must* have sent him off with his ears tingling! You are like your mother in that, Frazier; she always knew how to put a man in his place."

"Well, at least he knows how I feel about him," Frazier admitted.

CHAPTER
FOURTEEN

Wanted!

Early the following morning the Thanes left for Emigrant Creek. Esteban had been moving south steadily for the past few days with the flock, which now numbered about fifteen hundred head, a small band of sheep, comparatively, in that country.

In face of the threats that had been made they deemed it wise to keep the flock as far to the south as possible. Then, too, their best road into the Reserve was by way of Emigrant Creek cañon. There was grass enough in the cañon to feed the herd for a week.

It was Aaron's intention to hold the flock there until the first of the month and send it in as soon as his permit allowed. Once in the cañon, he believed his sheep would be out of harm's way. Anticipating such a move, he had searched for a way down to the floor of the cañon. This he had found, one that deer and antelope had made for themselves long before he had ever dreamed of Nevada.

The greater part of the day was consumed in moving the flock, for it was a wild, almost impassable country. The stream swung continually from one wall to the other, opening up, now and then, into little grass-covered flats.

On the creek, some distance below them, Newt Parr had a cabin. He had been mining on Emigrant Creek for four years. When he went out for supplies he followed the cañon down to Quinn River and got into Paradise or Eden by swinging around to the south.

Newt had once taken out a few thousand dollars from a stringer of decayed quartz. In fact it had been his success that had tempted Kincaid to try his luck farther up the creek. Newt's find had soon petered out, however, and Lin had found nothing at all. Lin had given up, but old Newt had stayed on, sinking his dollars in new tunnels and drifts.

Some whispered that it was not all his own money that he dropped there. In other quarters it was said that Cantrell was his grub staker. But why a man as shrewd as Big Jim should stick to Newt was beyond conception.

So, except for Newt, who seldom left his claim, and an occasional deer-hunter or two in the fall, no one ever was seen on Emigrant Creek. Aaron had met Newt several times while looking for a trail into the cañon.

The old prospector had made a great deal of Aaron. He had talked of assays and values and potential fortunes so glibly that Aaron had wondered to himself if he had not chosen the wrong path to wealth in going in for sheep.

Newt was well aware that he had mixed subtle poison, for he had prescribed an identical dose for many gullible men in his time. He had been many places and seen much that was strange and adventurous.

Naturally Aaron found him interesting. He had come away from his last visit in complete sympathy with Newt's dreams and ambitions, seeing in him just another honest old man like himself who had tasted the iron of misfortune.

He had spoken to Frazier about him, praising Newt's patience and honesty, and wondering to himself if the man's very innocence had not often stood in the way of his success.

Being on the creek to-day, Aaron could not forego spending an hour with Newt. So after leaving Esteban, Frazier and he rode west until they came to Parr's mine.

Newt was at home, as usual. Although he did not say so, he had known for hours that they were on the creek above him. He did his best to appear the honest old prospector of popular tradition.

Frazier was not sure whether she liked him or not, even though she found him quaint and picturesque. He seemed almost too obsequious to her.

"What a blessing it is to see a woman on Emigrant Creek at last," he beamed. "It takes me back, Miss Thane, it takes me back!"

He did not say to what.

Frazier suggested that she would go on and leave her father to follow when he was ready. This suited both Aaron and Newt.

"Follow the creek west until you come to Cottonwood Creek," he advised. "You can go up the

140

Cottonwood to within a mile or two of home. You'll find it easier than climbing out of the cañon." He cocked an eye at the sky. "It might blow some before evening. You'll be out of the wind, going home that away."

"Well, you have your talk out, Father," Frazier agreed. "Don't worry about me."

They waved her good-bye and she continued on down the cañon. The cañon widened several miles west of Parr's cabin and the creek clung to the southern wall.

Frazier found the country almost too wild to enjoy it. In another hour the sun had disappeared and the sky took on a forbidding appearance. Viewed from the depths of the cañon it was chilling, to say the least.

Horace Greeley, her mule, lifted his ears as the first breath of cool air swept down the creek.

"Go on, Horace," Frazier urged. "It's going to storm and I've no mind to be caught here."

Horace thought otherwise, and although the skies continued to darken and the wind freshened so much that the willows along the creek began to thrash to and fro, the mule refused to quicken his pace.

By the time she reached Cottonwood Creek, the darkness of early evening had fallen, although it was not later than five.

Gathering storm always brought thunder and lightning, back East. With increasing alarm she waited for the heavens to be rent asunder. Nothing of the sort occurred, however. But the skies continued to darken and the wind to increase until it tore down the cañon with a wild, soprano-like scream.

Horace began to roll his eyes fearfully as she turned toward the north. A mile north of Emigrant Creek the country opened up until there was only the fringe of willows and the tangled brush of the creek bottom between her and the raging wind.

The air was filled with sand. It got into her eyes and mouth. Once Horace stopped. Frazier did not urge him on, thinking it might be better to wait until the storm had passed. But when at the end of half an hour the wind was still rising, she determined to go on at any cost.

It was night in earnest now — black and impenetrable. A coyote barked sharply. Wheeling as he barked it sounded as though four or five animals were in the creek bottom just ahead. In her ignorance she jumped to the conclusion that they were wolves.

She knew better than to turn back. Certainly the road could not be more than a mile and a half to the north. Once she reached it she would have her back to the storm and be reasonably certain of finding her way home.

Horace was finally persuaded to go on. Frazier let him have his head, preferring to trust to his instinct rather than to her own eyes in the inky blackness.

The limb of a dead buckthorn struck her across the face and brought the blood. Her waist was soon ripped. She had long since lost her hat.

"Go on, Horace!" she cried whenever the mule held back.

She had no way of knowing how late it was. The storm was as wild as ever.

Frazier knew that as the creek neared the road the willows and underbrush thinned, until at the crossing itself the creek bottom was bare. Before Cèsar was shot she had ridden along Cottonwood Creek for short distances. She thought she would recognize certain spots, were she to see them again. Unfortunately her eyes were of little use to her.

As a matter of fact, she was nearer the road than she believed.

In a storm of this sort the coyotes take to cover. By now there were five or six in the brush ahead of her. Wildcats were there, too, all falling back before her slow advance.

They began to give ground grudgingly, knowing that the brush was thinning, but afraid to risk slinking past her.

The coyotes began to bark noisily now. Suddenly one, bolder than his fellows, rushed by her. Horace reared and threw her. She scrambled to her feet although her right ankle pained her terribly. She called to the mule; Horace was gone.

She searched about on the ground for a club with which to defend herself. Her fingers encountered a piece of willow, but it was so rotten that it broke even as she lifted it to test its stoutness.

She had never been quite so thoroughly frightened. When she got up she went on, but walking now and trying to avoid the stinging blows of the buckthorn and dead brush.

Her ankle was swelling rapidly.

"I can't go much farther," she groaned.

As she stopped to ease her pain she heard something plunging toward her. A huge form brushed by, and she screamed for help. It was only the mule, frightened out his wits by a wildcat that had jumped him.

Not knowing, she called again and again. She did not stop to ask herself who there was to answer her cry.

A streak of light had appeared along the western horizon, revealing low-scudding clouds, racing onward at express-train speed. Against that bar of light a man on horseback was silhouetted momentarily.

Frazier saw him. The man was hunched low to escape the biting blast and riding swiftly. Certainly he would not see her. He might hear, though, and she forced another frightened cry to her dry lips.

A handkerchief muffled the man's face. His eyes were bloodshot. Frazier saw him pause at the crest for a backward glance, steeling his eyes to meet the burning sand.

He was in great haste. This storm, for all its buffeting of him, was to his liking. The floor of the desert was being swept clean; no trail of man or beast left tell-tale sign to-night.

He had been seen at noon. Even before the storm had set in he had had warning that he was pursued. He had ridden swiftly, but Piñon was no match for the thin strands of wire that had carried news of his presence to Cantrell.

Since his mad flight from the Circle D on Chino Creek, Kincaid had ridden many miles, avoiding

Paradise Valley and the ranches along the Little Humboldt. He had hoped to reach Emigrant Creek from the west, by way of Quinn River. One of Chris Bridger's men had seen him as he paused to water his horse at noon.

The news of what had happened on Chino Creek had reached Paradise Valley that morning. It had been relayed promptly to Cantrell, and he in turn had notified Bridger. Bridger had immediately warned his men to look out for Kincaid and McCarroll.

The storm had intervened in Lin's behalf, but he knew well enough that trouble rode at his back. He gave Piñon a nudge and the horse dashed down the hard-packed road at breakneck speed to come up all atremble at the bank of the creek.

Piñon lowered his head to drink, but Lin pulled him up sharply; no time for drinking now!

The horse took but a step, however, when he stopped in his tracks, ears lifting and body tensing nervously.

Kincaid cursed to himself. How had they managed to get ahead of him? He put his hand to his ear and listened as he peered into the blackness ahead.

Seconds dragged by as he listened — precious seconds — and then, off to his right, he caught a call for help.

He scowled and shook his head. How could he stop? Perhaps it was only a ruse to ambush him.

He was about to go on when the call came again — clearer now for a brief lull in the storm. Kincaid's mouth tightened. He knew that cry had issued from a woman's throat.

145

"Got to stop now," he groaned as he sent Piñon in the direction from which the cry had come. Cupping his hands to his mouth he shouted: "Hello, there! Where are you?"

"Here! Here!" Frazier shouted back, lurching toward him.

"*My God!*" Kincaid gasped as he recognized her voice. "Frazier!" he shouted. "Where are you?"

"Lin! Lin!" he heard her answer.

Throwing caution to the winds, he broke off a piece of dead sage and managed to light it. He saw her and ran to her side. Before the sage burned out he saw how torn and disheveled she was. The scratch on her cheek had bled. For a moment he was almost afraid to ask her what had happened and how she came to be there in the creek bottom.

"Oh, God, I thank you," she gasped feebly. "It's a miracle, Lin, your finding me."

"We can thank Cantrell for that; it was not my intention to come this way," said he. "But how do you come to be here?"

He put out a hand to steady her.

"No, no," she said bravely enough, "I won't faint. I'll be all right in a minute."

"But you are hurt!"

"I turned my ankle. It's painful, but nothing more. I've been lost for hours. I was following the creek back to the road. Our flock is on Emigrant Creek. Mr. Parr suggested that this would be the best way home for me. I didn't know how terrible a sand storm could be. Then Horace had to throw me."

146

She shivered nervously.

"There must be wolves in this bottom. They've been barking at me for an hour," she went on.

"Just coyotes, I guess, ma'am," he drawled. "You sure you ain't hurt none?"

She shook her head and tried to laugh. "I was never so frightened. I guess Horace will find his way home. I almost wish he wouldn't."

"I wouldn't worry about him," Lin muttered. The mellow timbre of her voice thrilled him. The scratch which marred her cheek did not detract from her wild beauty in his eyes.

In some intangible way it seemed to bring them nearer each other. Unconsciously his mouth hardened as he thought of himself, the pursued, turned rescuer. What would she say when she learned that he was wanted?

He listened instantly for any sound that might warn him that his pursuers were near. Only the screaming of the wind reached his ears.

"I reckon we'd better go," he said. "Piñon will carry both of us."

"You've been away a long time, Lin," she reminded him as he reached out to help her into the saddle. "Jim Cantrell seemed terribly worried."

"Cantrell's worryin' over me has just begun," Lin answered as he turned to listen again.

Frazier noticed his suppressed excitement now.

"What is it?" she demanded anxiously.

"They're after me, and they're not far away."

"You mean that the law is after you? that you're wanted?"

"Yes. Cantrell and the Law are ridin' together for once. Flash and I are wanted, all right. If they catch us, we're goin' to have a mighty hard time provin' we're innocent."

"What do they say you have done?" Frazier gasped.

"Horse thief is the name they're tryin' to tack onto us. The horses Cantrell sent us to get were stolen. We were caught with them. Before the sheriff arrived we got away. This thing goes back to the killin' of that boy, here on Cottonwood Creek. That business ain't bein' overlooked the way some folks thought."

"This is terrible, Lin! Don't let them catch you. I always thought you knew more about that affair than you would admit."

"Well, we know who killed him, and Cantrell knows that we know. I couldn't say anythin' before, but I'm free to talk now. I'd better tell you; somethin' may happen to me."

"Oh, don't say that! As for telling me — is it necessary?"

"No, I guess it ain't at that; you know."

"And Flash?"

"I haven't seen him since we broke away. If anythin' happens to him it will be just somethin' more that Cantrell will have to square with me."

"Come, come!" Frazier exclaimed suddenly. "Why do we stand here wasting precious seconds when they mean everything to you? Why didn't you go on, Lin? Why did you ever stop at all?"

148

He smiled at her in the darkness. "You would have had me go on?" he asked. "I didn't know it was you who called."

"And still you stopped! You *would*, Lin. I shall not forget that."

He helped her into the saddle.

"The wind isn't blowing so wildly now," Frazier remarked.

"I've been noticin' that. Storm's almost over. I hope it holds on until we reach your place."

They soon drew away from the creek. Kincaid held her close as Piñon broke into a free-swinging stride that made light of the long desert miles.

The storm continued to abate and by the time they reached home the wind had dropped to just a strong breeze.

Frazier turned to him anxiously. "Don't go on, to-night," she pleaded. "Father will surely be here soon."

"I've been thinkin' of him," Lin nodded. "I wonder what he's goin' to say about me."

"Leave that to me, Lin," Frazier exclaimed. "Father and you have got to agree from now on."

She stopped short and her fingers tightened on Kincaid's arm. "There's someone coming," she whispered. "Maybe it's Father."

Lin shook his head a moment later.

"Five or six horses kickin' up that racket," said he. "This will be Cantrell and Bridger. They're comin' fast. You slip into the house. Don't show a light until they knock. Maybe they won't stop — but I'm thinkin' they will."

"And what's to become of you?" Frazier cried.

"I'll slip around to the barn. Have you got a gun in the house?"

"Yes, Cantrell's gun is still here," Frazier replied thoughtlessly.

"Cantrell's gun?" Lin exclaimed. "What are you doin' with his gun?"

Frazier tried to hurry him away without an explanation, but he refused to stir until she had told him how Big Jim's gun happened to be in her possession.

"Well, get it. Keep it near you; you may need it," he warned.

The posse was so near now that the beat of their horses' hoofs was sharp and clear.

"Go!" Frazier beseeched him. "And God bless you, Lin!"

CHAPTER
FIFTEEN

"I Won't Forget!"

Frazier pinned back her hair and washed the blood from her face in the darkness. She had barely finished when she heard men riding into the yard. Before she could light a lamp, they were pouring into the room, Cantrell and Bridger at their head.

They stopped on seeing her.

As soon as she had the lamp chimney in place she whirled on them with Cantrell's gun raised menacingly.

"Jim Cantrell, is it your habit to break into your neighbors' homes in this fashion?"

"Where's your father?" was Cantrell's reply, pretending not to see the gun she had levelled at him.

Frazier was not to be put off.

"I threatened to shoot you yesterday," she told him, "and I shall certainly do it to-night unless you leave this house."

Cantrell summoned a smile to his lips.

"That's sure a man size gun you got," said he.

"I'm glad you recognize it. You get out of this house and knock as you should. I'll decide whether I want to admit you or not."

Something in her eyes convinced him that she meant what she said.

"Come on, boys," he laughed. "We're gettin' altogether too rough."

"Pritty airy for a sheepman's kid," one of Bridger's men growled.

When they had made a mock show of asking for admittance, Frazier faced them a second time. "If you've anything to say to me, Mr. Cantrell," she exclaimed with the withering contempt he usually won from her, "say it quickly."

"Anythin' to oblige a lady," he replied with an oily smirk. "I take it your father ain't home."

"As I told you once before, I can speak for this family. What business have you with us?"

There was a new insolence in his manner to-night. He had come to the conclusion that he had nothing to gain by handling her with "kid gloves," as he had said to Bridger. He knew that the news he carried would hurt her and he was anxious to deliver it.

"Did anyone go past here to-night?" he asked pointedly, "a man on horseback, for instance? — a man by the name of Kincaid," he added.

Frazier tried to hold her eyes steady. She knew Cantrell was staring at her, trying to read her thoughts.

"No," she managed to say. "I haven't seen him! No one went by here that I know of."

"Nor stopped, eh?" Chris Bridger demanded.

There was an insinuation, a veiled suggestion, beneath his question that could not be misconstrued. Frazier turned on him with eyes flashing.

152

"Your words do credit to you, Mr. Bridger," she said icily. "I wonder if that is the respect you show your own daughters."

"Ain't no use flying off the handle like that," a man who was a stranger to Frazier cut in.

"That's right," Big Jim agreed as he pushed the other man forward. "Quimby is a deputy sheriff. He's got a warrant for Kincaid's arrest."

"Arrest?"

Frazier did her best to stimulate complete surprise. She succeeded so well that Cantrell was completely fooled.

"I thought you'd be a little surprised," he grinned. "That's why they didn't come back. He and McCarroll were caught with a string of stolen broncs in their possession. They never went to get the horses I sent 'em for."

"Oh, there must be some mistake!" Frazier exclaimed with almost genuine excitement.

"No mistake at all! They tried to rope me in by sayin' I'd sent 'em there to pick up horses from a brand no one ever heard of. I spiked that yarn in a hurry. If there was any doubt about their bein' guilty they killed it by sluggin' a man set to guard 'em and shootin' their way to liberty."

"I can't believe it!" Frazier gasped. "Surely they didn't kill anybody?"

Cantrell smiled inscrutably.

"Well, not in gittin' away, but I'm thinkin' it won't be long before folks around here will be puttin' two and two together about who killed Cèsar. Your father was the first one had that idea; I guess he knew what he was talkin' about."

"A man who'll steal horses will do most anythin'," Bridger agreed.

Frazier's face blanched with genuine horror now. "My father never accused them of killing Cèsar," she protested excitedly.

"No, but he was suspicious of them, and with good cause!" Big Jim declared.

"When did you hear they were wanted?" Frazier asked, hoping to trip him.

"Why, this mornin'!"

"Then why were you so sure yesterday afternoon that they were in trouble?"

This interested Quimby, the deputy from Elko County. Cantrell was caught without an immediate answer.

"It would almost seem as if you had connived against them," Frazier went on as Cantrell fumbled for words. "I know how little you liked them."

"That'll be about enough of that!" Cantrell roared. "I been suspicious of them a long time."

Frazier smiled to herself as she saw how the man had delivered himself into her hands.

"Yes, ever since the day that Cèsar was killed," she answered. "I don't mind saying that have always suspected you and Mr. Bridger. You were here that afternoon, prophesying trouble and making threats against the Basques. Why should you have suddenly turned against two men who had been working for you for such a long while?"

154

Cantrell was beside himself with rage. He could have killed her where she stood.

"Have you the impudence to accuse me of havin' had a hand in that boy's death?" Bridger demanded hotly, his white mustache on edge and an apoplectic purple tinging his round cheeks.

Frazier held her ground.

"I have the courage to say that I think you are just as open to suspicion as the two men whom you accuse," she declared.

"You'll pay for this," Bridger snorted impotently.

"I do not doubt but what we will. Mr. Cantrell warned me yesterday that it was time for us to 'git.' Fortunately, all of the cattlemen north of the Reserve are not like you."

This was touching a tender spot with Cantrell. He was gullible enough to believe that Wheeler might have said something to her.

"You'll get more than you're lookin' for," he blustered. "When you start accusin' men like Bridger and me, you're goin' too far."

"So, for all of your representations of friendship you'll turn on me as you have on your men," Frazier answered with cutting scorn "Evidently they knew what they were doing in escaping."

"Don't you be too sure they've escaped," Bridger growled. "You sheepmen are makin' hell enough without havin' horse-thieves added to our troubles. We're organized against that, ain't we boys?"

There was muttered approval of this from the others.

"I reckon that's just talk," the deputy volunteered. "They'll be caught and turned over to the law without any trouble. All of these northern counties will be posted by to-morrow."

He handed Frazier a poster offering a reward for the arrest of Kincaid and McCarroll and giving a description of both.

"They'll have to show themselves sooner or later," he continued. "If these men are guilty as charged, they'll be up to their old tricks again." He turned to Bridger. "I guess we can get along; the storm's over."

Cantrell hung back as they filed out.

"Kincaid was headin' this way when we last saw him," he muttered knowingly. "I allow he was comin' to see you."

"Don't be too sure that he was not coming to see you," Frazier flung back at him. "Knowing him as I do, I suspect he'll arrange to do that."

That very thought had occurred to Cantrell earlier in the day.

"Here is your gun," Frazier said as she handed the pistol to him. "You undoubtedly will need a gun."

Cantrell grinned at her with admiration now.

"You're a spitfire, ain't yuh?" said he. "That's all right with me. You'll be tame enough before long."

Frazier did not reply as he flung himself out of the room. A moment later she heard them riding away.

Now that they were gone, tears stole down her velvety cheeks. The last hours had been too much for her. Her faith in Lin needed no prop, but had one been necessary, Cantrell's haste to leap from this matter of the stolen horses to the killing of the herder would have supplied it. In itself it confirmed the very thing Lin had pointed out.

She was glad she had defied Cantrell. Nothing he could do could be worse than what he had already threatened to do. There was also good reason to believe that what she had said might give him pause, for although he was undoubtedly a coward, he was far from being a fool.

Frazier did not doubt that Cantrell and Bridger would find time before the night was out to discuss her attack. In fact, she believed that they had failed to search the house and barn only because of what she had said.

She glanced up quickly as she heard the kitchen door open. Lin was standing there. He appreciated fully what she had done for him.

"I guess you know what I'm up against now. It's my word against theirs for the present."

"Not with me, Lin; I know you are innocent. Cantrell did the very thing you told me he would — about Cèsar, I mean. But I gave him something to think about on his own account."

"Yes, I know, I was afraid they might search the barn, so I turned Piñon out and crawled back under the porch. I heard most all was said. You gave it to him straight and he'll either ride clear of you or hit you hard, now."

"We had nothing to gain by trying to placate him; you know that, Lin. But what are you going to do? I don't want anything to happen to you."

The mists which swam in her eyes sent his throat dry. He trembled as he felt himself caught up and held in its breathless grip. It left him tired and emphasized his loneliness.

"I've got a cabin on Emigrant Creek. I reckon I'll go there for a spell," he drawled softly.

"But won't they find you? You heard what Quimby said."

"He'll go back to Elko in a day or two. It's Cantrell and Bridger that I'll have to worry about. Flash went east when we separated. Chances are he's still in the Basin findin' out some things for himself. If I hadn't been worryin' myself sick tryin' to figure out why Cantrell wanted us out of the way for a week I'd never have walked into his trap. Flash didn't tumble either. We were taken in like two babies."

He gave her a detailed account of what had occurred.

"Cantrell must have had an accomplice," Frazier declared when he had finished.

"Of course! I'm hopin' Flash has found out somethin'. I told him I'd wait for him on Emigrant Creek. So you see I've got to stay there for a while."

"You'll need food," Frazier remarked.

"I'll get that at Eden. I'm not known there. I'll make a bluff at minin' while I'm on the creek. If any stranger drops in on me I'll have sort of an excuse for bein' on the creek."

"I guess you will see very few strangers there," Frazier smiled wanly. "It's too wild for that. But our

158

boy Esteban is on the creek with the flock. Mr. Parr is there, too."

"That Basque boy won't make me any trouble," Lin assured her. "He'll be movin' into the Reserve next Monday, if your father gets his permit."

"He has it already," Frazier exclaimed. "Father intends sending our sheep into the Reserve at the earliest possible moment."

"He's wise to do it, although he's liable to have trouble gettin' them in. That's another reason why I want to be on the creek. As for Newt Parr, I'll take mighty good care to stay out of *his* way."

"Why what about Mr. Parr?" Frazier asked.

"Nothin'," Lin replied, "other than that he and Cantrell are friends. I hope your father won't find it necessary to tell Newt about me."

"I'll see to that," Frazier assured him. "I know you would stop at nothing in our behalf, Lin. But I hope you will not have to risk your liberty over our sheep."

"Well, I guess I'll get along," said he, opening the door behind him. "It may take me a little time to find Piñon."

Frazier gave him her hand.

"Good-bye," she whispered. "And don't worry about Father; I'll explain everything to him. Father is apt to—"

She stopped short on seeing that Lin was not listening.

"Somebody comin'," said he.

"Don't go, then!" she exclaimed with quick alarm. "It may be Cantrell returning."

"I reckon it's your daddy this time," Lin drawled. "Chances are that he has met up with Cantrell and the others. He'd hardly understand my bein' here, so I'll get along."

It seemed the wise thing to do. Frazier gave him her hand again and her eyes held his tenderly.

"Good-bye, Lin," she murmured. "Remember, you are very dear to me."

"Ma'am," said he, so softly that she barely heard, "I promise you I won't forget!"

CHAPTER
SIXTEEN

"Your Turn Next!"

Kincaid's presence in the little town of Eden the following day went unnoticed. By evening he was on his way back to Emigrant Creek with supplies enough to last him for a month.

He was careful to cut down into the cañon far above Newt Parr's shack. The little flats that he crossed as he continued up the creek told him that Aaron's flock was moving toward the Reserve, for the grass had been grazed to the roots.

"They'll have to do some scratchin' to find their breakfast, come Monday mornin', the way they're cleanin' out everythin' in sight," Lin drawled aloud. "Hardly feed enough on the creek to keep a flock as big as that goin' for three or four days."

He judged Esteban must have moved up almost abreast his old cabin. It was his intention to speak to Esteban in the morning and swear the boy to secrecy, counting on the Basque's fear and hatred of Cantrell more than on his loyalty to the Thanes for his silence.

The bare spots on the flats were deep with dust where the flock had passed.

Kincaid came up with a start a few minutes later as he caught sight of the clear-cut impressions of shod hoofs in the dust. He knew where Aaron and Frazier had entered the cañon. He was more than a mile above that spot now.

Even by moonlight he could see that whoever had made those tracks had ridden at a gallop. That was more disturbing than the tracks themselves.

He brought his horse to a walk and moved ahead cautiously, trying to keep to the deep shadows along the southern wall, looking for sign as he moved on.

The tracks continued. He searched the narrowing cañon but caught no glimpse of any moving object.

He came within sight of the old cabin at last. He straightened suddenly, his lips twitching nervously as he realized that the tracks which he was following were heading directly for his cabin.

He asked himself if Cantrell could have got wind of his plan to come back to Emigrant Creek and settle down under the very nose of the Lazy K. It seemed impossible. Only Frazier had been taken into his confidence.

Gun in hand, he swung to the ground and picked his way toward the cabin door. The moonlight was just touching it.

His eyes dilated as he stared at the door. Someone had left a message there. It was just a dirty piece of paper, and the words it bore had been scrawled with the burnt end of a stick.

They were cryptic, grim!

162

Perspiration broke on Kincaid's forehead as he read the three words:

YOUR TURN NEXT!

For the moment he did not doubt that the message had been left there for him. Had they got Flash? Was that its significance?

He circled around to the rear and left Piñon. The place had but one window. He peered in cautiously. He could see nothing. The door had no lock. He poked it with the barrel of his gun and sent it flying back on its rusty hinges.

It was dark inside. He thought something moved on the floor — or was it just his nerves?

He listened — tense — a tingling of his blood at the roots of his hair. Plainly, then, he caught the sound of something moving in the darkness.

"Freeze!" he whipped out dreadfully, "or I'll bust you!"

His body steeled itself for the expected attack; but the noise stopped.

Kincaid's eyes were becoming accustomed to the darkness. He could see the crawling thing before him now. It was a man, bound, gagged, his face battered and bleeding.

Lin swore as he put his gun away, thinking it was Flash who lay on the floor before him. He struck a light, then.

A mingled gasp of relief and astonishment was wrung from him as he saw that it was not McCarroll.

"Esteban!" he muttered. "Evidently Cantrell was not bluffin' last night."

He got out his knife and removed the gag from the boy's mouth.

"What happened to you, *muchacho?* You look as if a mountain had fell on yuh!"

Esteban rolled his eyes fearfully.

"Man — beeg man — jomped me, *Señor*," he groaned wearily. "*Madre de Dios! Señor*, that man keeck hard!"

"Who was it?" Lin demanded impatiently.

"*Quien sabe?* Who knows? Hees boot wak' me up, but right away eet poot me back to sleep again."

He rubbed his jaw and felt of the swollen cheek where a boot-heel had cut deep.

Lin lighted a candle.

"Looks as though you've been livin' here," said he, not too well pleased.

"*Si, Señor*. The *Señor* Thane don't say not to stay here."

Kincaid got to his feet with an unpleasant laugh. The word Thane recalled the warning nailed to the door. He understood it now; it was meant for Frazier's father.

"Where are your sheep?" Lin asked.

"I leave them in that leetla basin like where the cañon widens out just above here. But theese man what comes ees go up there. I hear heem shoot. *Por Dios!* who knows where those sheep ees now?"

"You say it was a big man. Was it Cantrell?"

Esteban did not answer.

164

"Was it Cantrell?" Lin demanded angrily. "Answer me!"

The boy cowered before him. "How I know that, *Señor?*" he whimpered.

Kincaid turned away with an oath, certain that Esteban knew who had beaten him, but was afraid to tell.

Esteban tried to untie the ropes that bound him.

"I'll cut 'em," Lin grumbled. "I ought to leave you tied up, though. You know who beat you."

"But no, *Señor!* I was told to hold the flock here until Monday, when we put them on the Reservation. Some mens not like that. But who?" He shrugged his shoulders eloquently. "How I know that?"

Groaning loudly he crawled to the bunk which stood in the corner. Kincaid stared at him ominously for a minute.

"Esteban," he drawled unpleasantly, "I suspect you are a damned liar. You could give me an answer if you wanted too. When a couple of your friends get banged up, maybe you'll change your mind." Lin turned away disgustedly. "Whoever it was," he exclaimed, "he's still on the creek. I aim to have a look at him."

"Don't go!" Esteban cried as Kincaid reached the door. "He say he ees come back before he go. Eef he find me untied he keel me sure!"

Lin stopped and stared at him sharply.

"Are you lyin'?" he demanded.

Before the boy could answer, Kincaid caught the patter of hoofs.

Esteban crossed himself and began to whimper again.

"Get under the bed or the stove," Lin flung at him. "I'll run this show from now on!"

The man on horseback came abreast the dugout. Lin heard him stop. He dropped to his knees at the window and gripped his Colts.

Bang! bang! bang! rang out a fusillade as the man outside shot out the windows and riddled the door.

Esteban screamed. Kincaid heard the rider chuckle.

"Tell it to Thane!" the man shouted derisively as he rode off.

Kincaid leaped to his feet. He would have known that voice anywhere.

It was Cantrell's!

He was already some yards away. Lin sent a shot after him for luck. A mocking laugh floated back, but his Stetson sailed into the air.

Big Jim did not stop to recover it, but raked his horse with his spurs and soon passed from view down the cañon.

Lin found the hat a few minutes later. He carried it back to the dugout and examined it. Stamped in the sweathband were Cantrell's initials.

Esteban had crept out from underneath the bed. Lin tossed the hat to him.

"You read?" he inquired sharply. Esteban shook his head. "J.A.C. is what those initials say. That hat belongs to Jim Cantrell. You ready to talk, now?"

Kincaid glared at him so fiercely that he fell back a step.

"*Si, Señor,*" he exclaimed fervently. "It was Cantrell who keecked me!"

"Of course it was! Now you get your stuff together and get out of here. I'm goin' to live here from now on. You drift up to the basin where you left your sheep, and stay with 'em. I'm goin' up there now and have a look. I'll keep on up into the Reserve and get over the hills and down to the Thanes. And remember this, Esteban, if you're at all fond of livin', keep your mouth shut about my bein' here!"

"I tell no wan, *Señor,*" Esteban promised. "I thought Cantrell and you was great friend," he ventured. "You work for heem, eh?"

"No more," Kincaid answered curtly. "If Newt Parr happens to come snoopin' around here, forget that you know how to talk English — even the kind that you talk. You understand?"

"*Si!*" Esteban exclaimed with a nod of understanding. "The *Señor* Thane blame me, I suppose, for what ees happen tonight," he added miserably.

"Well, you should have stayed with the flock; but you couldn't have stopped Cantrell. I'll tell them so. You come here in the mornin'; I may have some word for you."

It took him only a few minutes to reach the flock. He knew well what to expect, but he cursed himself as he saw the result of Cantrell's handiwork.

"I reckon I'm to blame for this," he ground out savagely. "She shouldn't have stood up for me that-a-way. I hate sheep, but I've got to look out for this bunch from now on."

He wondered what effect this incident would have on Aaron's feeling toward him. He was far from convinced that Frazier could win over her father. And yet, for all the risk that the trip entailed, and regardless of how Aaron Thane received him, he had to acquaint him with what had happened.

At best he could not hope to arrive at the ranch much before midnight. There was no hint of a trail up the creek.

He rubbed Piñon's ears affectionately.

"You've got to use your head as well as your laigs to-night, old timer," he murmured. "It'll be daylight before we get back here — if we're lucky enough to get back at all. It's up to you."

CHAPTER
SEVENTEEN

A New Understanding

Kincaid made better time than he had counted on and it was but a few minutes after eleven when he came in sight of the Thane place. He saw that a light burned brightly in the parlor. Leaving the road some distance east of the house, he approached by way of the barn.

He had hardly expected to find them awake at this late hour. Unless some festivity was in progress, a light at this time of night in that country was usually cause for misgiving.

Leaving Piñon at the barn, Lin picked his way to the kitchen door. A moment later the front door was opened and Newt Parr came out. Lin drew back into the shadows. What was Newt doing here at such an hour? he asked himself. He resolved to find out before he left.

When he knocked a few moments later, Frazier opened the door. She fell back in surprise on recognizing him.

"Lin!" she gasped, "has something happened to you?"

Her concern moved Kincaid mightily.

"No, ma'am," he murmured, "there's nothin' to worry about on my account."

"But it's dangerous for you to come here. I know you would not have risked it for nothing."

"That's true, of course," he answered as Aaron came into the kitchen.

Frazier's father recognized him at once, and Lin drew himself up rather stiffly, wondering what Aaron would say. To his surprise, the old man offered him his hand.

"I guess we've misunderstood each other," said he. "Frazier has told me all about these charges against you."

"And Father thinks they are as absurd as I do," Frazier smiled. "Don't you, Father?"

He nodded, but he could not help arching his eyebrows a little at her. Her defense of Lin had not left him a leg to stand on, even though he had hung out long after he had secretly admitted that she had made her point.

"I'm mighty glad to hear you say that," Lin said gratefully.

Now that Aaron had come to look on Kincaid in a new light it did not seem strange that Frazier should have championed his cause. There was something about the man that radiated confidence in his ability to meet any issue — that rare mixture of smile and steel that he had always ascribed to the gallant Sheridan, under whom he had once served.

"I was going to look you up to-morrow," Aaron declared. "I don't know how you feel about it, but if Cantrell killed that boy he ought to be brought to justice. The man fooled me completely at first, but I'm

170

beginning to understand him and appreciate his power. We've got to make an example of him."

"Well, I've got some ideas along those lines myself," Lin admitted, "but if we're to win, we've got to outsmart him. Don't rely on the law; the law won't help us at all. I'll go to jail and you'll be broke if we try to beat him that way."

"How do you propose to go about it, then?" Aaron demanded skeptically, unwilling to admit that they could not obtain legal justice.

"By beatin' him at his own game. One of these days he'll be at the end of the plank and afraid to jump."

Frazier pulled down the window shades.

"Cantrell may be watching the house," she explained as her father gave her a questioning glance.

"Or Newt Parr," Lin muttered.

Aaron threw up his head at this. For a moment Frazier feared all her work had been undone.

"What is the matter with Newt Parr?" Aaron demanded. "You shouldn't be suspicious of every man in the country."

"I'm suspicious of anyone who is friendly with Cantrell," Lin declared flatly.

"You're mistaken about Parr," Aaron exclaimed. "He never mentioned Cantrell to-night."

"And yet while he was here keepin' you engaged, your flock was raided. That's what I came to tell you. Esteban has been banged up and not less than twenty-five head of sheep slaughtered."

"Who did it?" Aaron cried, utterly aghast.

"Cantrell! There's his hat."

Frazier was far the calmer of the two as Lin related his story. Old Aaron paced the floor with mounting anger, a baffled look in his eyes. He could not believe that Newt Parr knew aught of this outrage.

"Get my boots!" he exclaimed, "I'll go to the creek at once."

"No need of doin' that," said Lin. "I'm goin' back now. The trouble has been done for to-night. I feel as bad over this as you do. If you hadn't stuck up for me, why—"

"Don't say that, Lin," Frazier begged. "Cantrell threatened to do something of the sort when he was here day before yesterday." She had told her father of that incident in order to win him over.

"Yes, he's ordered us to get out," Aaron agreed. "I don't blame you for this. Twenty-five head killed!" he groaned. "Has the boy been hurt?"

"He'll be all right," Lin declared.

"Is it possible that Cantrell can commit one crime after another and never be made to pay for them?" Frazier asked.

"He'll pay," Lin muttered tersely. "I'm in this to the finish, but my hand must not be seen. Cantrell won't be so crude with me."

"He'll find I won't quit, either," Aaron exclaimed. "I'll move my sheep Monday morning as I said I would. Once I get them on government land, he'll have to keep his hands off."

"I hope so," Lin replied without much encouragement. "I wouldn't look for any help from the rangers; they'll keep out of this fight if they can."

172

"What would you do now?" Frazier asked.

"Watch the flock carefully. Cantrell will strike again before Monday mornin'. To-morrow's Sunday. You can send the flock in after midnight. That might fool him." He paused to turn to Aaron. "Do you want my advice, Mr. Thane?" he asked.

"Of course we do," Frazier answered for her father. "We need your help, Lin. It's because we are so green at this business that Cantrell is sure he can discourage us. But we will not be driven out."

Kincaid wondered what she would have said had he told her about the warning on his dugout door.

"We couldn't pull out if we wanted to," Aaron declared emphatically. "Almost all the money I've got is invested here. If you've got any advice to give, Kincaid, I'll listen to it."

"Well, you and Miss Frazier go up to see Esteban to-morrow. Stop for a word with Parr. It won't do any harm to tell him just what you want him to know. Let on that you're up for the day only; that you're goin' to move the flock Monday mornin'."

Lin saw that Aaron did not take kindly to his continued suspicion of Newt.

"It don't hurt to lie a little, no matter how honest you think a man is, not when you're expectin' trouble," he insisted. "Don't mention my name; be sure of that. I'll get over the hills now and clean up my place so the two of you can stay there tomorrow night. Esteban was usin' the dugout; I made him get out."

"Of course we'll come to the creek to-morrow," Aaron assured him. "I'm sorry you're suspicious of

173

Parr," he continued. "He came here to-night to show me a piece of rich ore he has just taken out. I'm anxious to inspect his mine."

"But where is this scheming going to bring us?" Frazier questioned wearily.

Kincaid smiled at her. "It ain't really what you might call schemin'," said he; "it ain't sure enough to be called that. My idea is that as soon as you get to the dugout we'll move the flock up into that narrow pass just this side of the Reservation line. We can hold them there. I'll get above them and you folks can stay below. No one can get by us then without our knowin' it. If nothin' happens to stop us, we'll send them into the Reserve sharp at midnight."

"There's sense in what you say," Aaron admitted. "We'll be where we can watch our sheep."

"Cantrell will need as much watchin' as the flock," Lin admonished him. "That's why I don't want Parr to know you are stayin' on the creek for the night. Of course if he's spyin' for Cantrell, he'll get word to him that you haven't gone out. I'm hopin' that news may reach him too late to cause us any trouble, for make no mistake about it, Cantrell will be on the creek by sunup Monday mornin', representin' for all he's worth. What time can I expect you?"

"We'll be there by noon," Aaron informed him.

"I'll count on you," said Lin as he caught up his hat. The night was mild.

"I'll walk to the barn with you," Frazier volunteered. "I'll get some sugar for Piñon."

"Good-night, Kincaid," her father exclaimed as they closed the door.

"I'm sorry you have to ride the rest of the night," Frazier murmured as Piñon munched his sugar.

"Ridin' at night is sorta soothin' to me," Lin smiled. "You haven't seen this country until you've looked at it by moonlight."

"I should love to see it by moonlight some time," she answered softly — "with you."

Once back on Emigrant Creek he could, and most undoubtedly would, appreciate this statement at its true worth, but he was too near the divine presence at the moment to be anything other than harassed and embarrassed by her interest in him.

Frazier suspected as much and enjoyed his discomfiture.

"Haven't seen anythin' of Flash, yet," he drawled as he got into his saddle. "I hope he shows up soon."

"So do I," said Frazier. "I might borrow his horse."

She gave Lin a smile that was well calculated to add to the sweet misery that gripped him. "Piñon has carried the two of us before," he remarked with surprising boldness.

It was Frazier who was on the defensive now.

"Not to-night," she sighed tenderly. "Good-night! You've a long way to go, Lin."

He knew he was being dismissed, and he knew nought to do but go.

Thought of her stayed with him as he rode along. He found the mystery, called woman, quite as hard to understand as have so many others.

CHAPTER
EIGHTEEN

"That's My Answer!"

A majestic stillness rested upon the fastnesses of Emigrant Creek the next morning as Frazier and her father followed the broken trail that led to Kincaid's cabin.

The ragged rimrocks, high above the floor of the cañon, seemed softened, even unreal against the deep turquoise of the cloudless sky. It was as though the inanimate ledges and brooding trees recognized that this was the Lord's Day.

It was chastening. Frazier was reminded of many church-going Sunday mornings back in Great Barrington.

Newt Parr, who was aware of their presence on the creek long before they came abreast of his place, was not similarly affected. In fact, he cursed most loudly. He wanted Aaron to see his mine — indeed that was his chief concern — but the mine was not yet ready for a formal "at home."

Newt had plenty of time in which to make up his mind as to what he wanted to do about meeting Aaron. He finally decided to take himself off, so when the Thanes arrived they found the shack deserted.

"Gone to Paradise, no doubt," Aaron exclaimed, apparently relieved. "We will not have to stretch the truth about our visit, now. I wouldn't want him to think that we distrusted him."

Frazier smiled indulgently, wondering if he was not too easily swayed in his judgment of men. She said nothing, however, and they continued up the creek.

Lin was waiting for them. He was fresh-looking although he had slept but an hour or two.

This wild, rugged land fitted him. Her pulse quickened as she gave him her hand and felt the answering pressure of his fingers.

"Knew you were comin' for some time; I could hear you talkin', it's so still."

"Came right along," Aaron assured him. "Parr's place was deserted."

"Strange, him bein' away like that," Lin mused. "He wouldn't go out for grub on Sunday."

"It serves our purpose that he isn't home," Aaron declared. "No one knows that we are here now."

"He'll know if he gets back," said Lin. "He's desert bred; he can read signs."

"Where's Esteban?" Aaron asked. "I am anxious to see the flock."

"I want you to have a bite to eat before you go up," Lin hastened to say.

"I'm ravenously hungry," Frazier exclaimed. "I smell coffee!"

"There's a pair of sage-chickens to go with it, too," Lin smiled. "Esteban was here an hour ago. He is limpin' badly and his face is out of kilter, but he's on the job."

Aaron was staring at the bullet-riddled door. "The man must be mad," he muttered to himself as he turned away. He found something more discouraging in this mute evidence of Cantrell's senseless rage than in the killing of his sheep.

Lin had cleaned the dugout thoroughly. Frazier remarked the fact. She did her best to make the meal a pleasant one, but her father had little to say.

Lin saddled Piñon when they had finished eating.

"You had better stay here," he advised Frazier. "Your father will be back shortly. I'll go on up above. If anyone comes, which is likely, Cantrell or Bridger, for instance, and insists on going into the basin, you follow them. There's a rifle in the corner, there. If you leave the cabin, take the gun with you. If you need me, shoot; the sound will carry as far as the pass."

"I hope that will not be necessary," Frazier murmured as she glanced at her father. "You don't intend to move the flock right away?"

"No, not until evenin'. Esteban and I will get them in the pass about sunset and hold them there until after dark. Uncle Sam won't be hurt any if we move into the Reserve an hour or two before time."

Aaron was already fifty yards away. Lin was about to follow him when he turned back for a moment. "There's one thing more," said he. "If Cantrell shows up, you do the talkin'."

The day wore on without anything untoward happening. Aaron had returned promptly. Frazier tried her best to cheer him up. "Everything will be all right, Father," she said encouragingly. "We can rely on Lin."

"I know we can," he admitted. "He would make a go of this business where I never could. I'm beginning to wonder if I didn't make a mistake."

"Of course you didn't! We've just got to make a success of it."

"Of course! Of course!" he agreed as he went out to inspect Lin's old tunnels, but he knew that if he had it to do over again he would do differently. Newt Parr's stories of the wealth that lay underground, just waiting for man to claim it, were having the desired effect.

Newt had returned to his cabin soon after the Thanes had passed. There, an hour later, Cantrell joined him. He had been drinking, but Newt's news sobered him quickly.

"Goin' to be on hand to run their sheep in first thing in the mornin', eh?" he mocked. "By God! I'll spoil that little game! At that, I bet it was her idea, not his."

He cursed violently and pulled his mustache. But he went to no great effort in deciding what to do.

"You've got to get them back here, Newt," he declared. "Tell the old man that you saw his trail — shucks! You know what to tell him. Flash a piece of ore on him. Accordin' to you, he's ready to take the hook in that direction."

Newt nodded. "I don't suppose it would do any good to ask what you intend doing in the meantime?"

Cantrell grinned as usual.

"You'll know soon enough," said he.

Half an hour later Parr's hearty greeting brought Aaron to the door of Lin's dugout. Newt claimed to have made another find at his mine. His excitement over his own good fortune seemed so genuine that even Frazier was fooled.

There was no mention made of their business on the creek, other than that they were waiting for Esteban. So, when Parr begged them to go down to his cabin, they had no valid excuse for refusing.

"But Esteban is in the basin," Frazier protested. "He will come here and wait. One of us ought to remain."

"Ain't no need of that," Newt insisted. "Waiting is one of the best things a Basque does. You-er ain't expecting trouble from anyone, are you?" he asked with grave concern.

He had put her on the defensive so adroitly that, think what she might, she could do nothing but say no. The next moment she turned the tables on him, however.

"What made you think we might be expecting trouble?" she asked lightly.

Newt's eyebrows lifted at the question. Only his thoroughly disarming smile saved him.

"Always trouble where sheep and cattle are fighting for range," said he. "Not that I've heard anything — don't let me frighten you. As Holy Writ says, there's no tongue so bad as an idle one."

In the end he won them over.

Cantrell, from his hiding place in the tangled malpais, smiled his satisfaction as he saw them start down the cañon. Once they had passed him, he went directly to the dugout.

The very neatness of the place which Lin had contrived that morning, angered him. He took a savage delight in turning everything upside down. Some minutes passed before he had vented his spleen completely.

His eyes were red with hate as he came to the door and tested the wind with a moistened finger.

"Blowin' strong enough right now," he said gruffly. "No use waitin' for it to stiffen. It may turn in another hour."

Fifty yards above the dugout the sage-brush grew thickly. Everything was parched.

Cantrell knew all this; he was playing a sure thing this time. Five minutes after he had applied a match to a tiny pile of dry sage the flames were racing toward the basin.

The oily sage and greasewood roared as the fire consumed it. Angry tongues of flame leaped ten feet high in places.

Cantrell laughed with fiendish glee as he watched the line of fire traveling up the cañon faster than a man could walk.

Clouds of black smoke began to rise. The freshening wind did the rest. "That'll hold you," Cantrell cried as he shook his fist in the direction of Aaron's flock. "You can graze your sheep in hell, now!"

He had left his horse on the rimrocks. The ascent was difficult. He stopped a few feet below the rimrocks to look back at his handiwork. He could see the basin, all aflame now.

"That's my answer," he muttered. "You wanted trouble and you got it!"

The smoke was thick even at that height. He paused but for a moment. The last twenty feet of the wall rose sheer. Once or twice he wondered if he could make the top. The rock was so rotten that it crumbled often as he put his weight on it. Whenever he found a spot that looked strong enough to bear him, he explored it gingerly, not knowing when his hand might close upon a rattlesnake, sunning itself.

Every step upward made it more imperative that he reach the top, for he knew he could never make his way down again. A faint drumming in the sky told him that the rangers had noted the smoke and were flying toward the cañon. He had no desire to be seen. Desperation made him bold and he reached the top nearly exhausted, a few minutes later; but his sigh of relief was quickly smothered, for spread out over the plateau, which stretched away to the south, were thousands of sheep. He knew they were being moved up to go on the Reserve.

This was Basque range. Cantrell could see the herders and men on horseback less than a quarter of a mile away. They had noticed the smoke and were hurrying toward the cañon. He knew what was likely to happen if he was caught there.

He could see the rangers' plane now, soaring nearer. That decided him. His horse was two hundred yards away. He ran toward it for all he was worth.

182

One burly figure had detached itself from the group of herders and was riding rapidly in his direction. Cantrell recognized the man for Irquieaga. He had sworn vengeance on the big Basque, but he found flight the better part of valor to-day, and he leaped into his saddle and fled without a backward glance.

CHAPTER
NINETEEN

Smoke and Fire

From the moment that Aaron Thane had shown interest in Newt Parr's mine it had been Newt's intention to sell him an interest in the property. With that in mind, he had planned to salt it. This had not been done as yet, so it was with some misgiving that he showed the mine to Aaron and Frazier to-day. He saw soon enough that he had nothing to fear, for Frazier knew as little about mining as her father. He glowed accordingly.

Aaron found the mine and Newt's talk of values at hand of absorbing interest. Frazier was frankly disappointed. She had expected to see yellow gold. Perhaps this black, silver-pricked quartz, which Newt pointed to so proudly, was worth a potential fortune, but it carried no thrill to her eyes.

Newt talked at such length that he wearied her, and due to her urging they came to the surface. Words froze on their lips as their nostrils dilated with acrid smoke, clouds of which shut them in.

Aaron's face went white. Frazier stared at Parr, searching his eyes for some sign of guilt.

Old Newt was too good an actor to be caught in that fashion. In fact, he became their champion and led the mad flight up the cañon.

"All my fault," he wailed as he berated himself. "Didn't have no business getting you folks to come here to listen to my troubles. Now some skunk has set fire to the grass and trapped your sheep! As if there wasn't room enough for all!"

He pointed to the circling plane.

"Here come the rangers already!"

Frazier glanced up at the plane. What could the rangers do? She saw that her father was crushed and silent in the face of this fresh calamity.

Horace Greeley, the mule, snorted as the smoke began to bother him. Frazier leaped to the ground and ran ahead on foot.

She had come to share Kincaid's distrust of old Newt. He was too interested, too servile.

Aaron was the first to reach the dugout. He was at the point of saying that Lin was not there when Frazier stopped him. She realized that she had to get rid of Newt.

"I wish you would let us go on alone, Mr. Parr," she exclaimed. "It's kind of you to offer to help; but our enemies are unscrupulous enough to stop at nothing. There is no need of involving you."

Newt's eyes narrowed shrewdly as he studied her. He turned away to view the smouldering, blackened ruin the fire had left.

"I am afraid we *are* too late," said he, even though he pretended to insist on offering his help.

185

"There are powerful interests at work here, my friend," Aaron warned him. "Go home; I'll stop for a word on the way out."

Frazier threw her arms around her father's neck as soon as they were alone.

"Don't give way, Father," she pleaded, trying her best to be brave. "We can make a fresh start even though we lose the whole flock."

"I know, Frazier," he answered dully. "We must keep our heads up. Kincaid warned us, but I didn't think Cantrell or Bridger would go this far. It'll be some time before we can get into the basin. I hope the boy and Kincaid were not trapped there."

Frazier gasped at this. It had not occurred to her that Lin might have been caught by the fire.

Aaron felt her go limp in his arms. In turn he became the stronger of the two.

"There's nothing to do but wait until the smoke rises. Even the rangers are going back."

"He may be lying up there, charred, unrecognizable, because of his devotion to us," she sobbed. "We can never forgive ourselves; he warned us not to leave the cabin."

Aaron led her inside where she fell to her knees and prayed earnestly. It well may be that in answer to her supplication Heaven lent strength to the man for whom she prayed. Certain it is that Kincaid never toiled with greater determination.

He had no sooner reached the basin that afternoon than Esteban and he began to move the flock. By the time the fire became menacing, Aaron's sheep were flowing up the pass that led to the Reserve.

Esteban's dog had given them their first hint of danger. The boy had wanted to run, but Lin had held him back with the direst of threats. Esteban's difficulties increased as the smoke and flames began to send the flock wild.

The droning of the plane overhead did not help the situation.

"They can't land," Lin cursed. "Why don't they pull out?"

The rangers opened their chemical tank and a fine spray began to fall. It seemed to have no effect at all.

"Nothin' but backfirin' goin' to stop this," Lin muttered bitterly.

The rangers evidently came to that conclusion, too, for the plane soon withdrew.

Kincaid's backfires grew, but the perverse wind caused new fires to start in back of him. The heat became so intense that he almost dropped.

The fires he had started and the onrushing furnace met finally. With brain reeling, he dragged his weary body to the cañon wall. There, in a crevice, he waited. He knew this was the test. Either the two fires would fight each other until they burned themselves out, or the flames would circle past him and rush up the pass into the Reserve.

He lay there for fully half an hour as the fiery battle raged about him. He got to his feet a few minutes later as a breath of cooler air fanned his face. He knew he had won the fight. He tried to smile, but his parched and cracked lips refused to answer.

With danger past he found time to wonder how Cantrell, or whoever had started the fire, had managed to slip by Frazier and her father. The thought that they had been attacked occurred to him. He had heard no shooting, however.

He was anxious to get back to the dugout to learn what had happened, but he had first to talk to Esteban.

"You save the flock, *Señor*," the boy exclaimed with genuine admiration. Esteban wondered how he managed to go on.

"You keep the flock in the pass until this evenin'," Lin ordered. "These rangers will be back here soon enough, on foot this time, to see that the fire doesn't get into the Reserve. If they ask, tell 'em you put it out. Don't say anythin' about me — and don't try to move the flock before dark, because they may be expectin' you to do that, and they'll stop you. You understand, Esteban?"

He nodded that he did, but to satisfy himself, Lin made him repeat his orders. With this attended to, Kincaid turned back to the dugout.

Frazier was the first to see him. A cry of relief escaped her as she ran to his side. He was actually staggering by now.

"Lin, Lin!" she exclaimed, "you are alive!"

"Yeh, I ain't dead yet," he managed to grin.

"It was all our fault," she went on. "Parr came to the dugout and got us to look at his mine."

188

She felt the rebuke in his eyes. "How can you ever forgive us?" she gasped. Aaron came to the door. "Father, Father!" she called to him. "He's here — alive!"

Aaron Thane's heart smote him sorely as he saw Kincaid's condition. For the first time all doubt of the man's loyalty vanished. He was so moved that he could not bring himself to ask about his sheep.

Kincaid heard in detail the story of their trip to the mine. But she was safe. Nothing else really mattered. He could be tired now.

They put him to bed, treated his burns as best they could and pressed cold water to his lips.

He slept for a while. They were seated beside him when he awoke.

"I must 'a' been just about licked," he murmured. He started to get up, but Frazier forced him back.

"You must be ravenous by now," she declared. "I'll cook supper for you."

Lin smiled his thanks. It thrilled him to think of her doing for him.

"I'm almost afraid to ask about the flock," Aaron said. "And the boy?"

"Esteban is all right and so is the flock."

"What?" Aaron exclaimed incredulously. "The sheep escaped?"

"Yes. We had the flock in the pass before the fire got bad. I talked to Esteban before I came down. He'll hold your sheep there until it gets dark."

Frazier came back to listen as he told them the story of the fight he had waged so successfully. When he had eaten and Frazier had succeeded in rolling a cigarette for him he was more like himself.

"I feel as though I was livin' again," he grinned. "You folks ought to be goin' home. I'll be able to go up and stay with the boy a while to-night."

Both protested against leaving him.

"But Parr will be lookin' for you. I don't want him to come snoopin' in here. You go home. He'll get a word with you. Tell him anythin' you please; it can't matter much now; the flock will be on the Reserve before any more trouble comes. I just don't want him to know about me."

"But you shouldn't get up," Frazier declared earnestly.

"What more can you do for me?" Lin asked.

Aaron had gone out.

"I don't suppose we can ever do enough to repay you for what you have done to-day," Frazier murmured as she smiled wistfully at him. "I want you to know that we appreciate it," she went on, placing her hand tenderly upon his forehead.

Kincaid looked away, mute for the moment.

"You may not think so, ma'am," he murmured finally. "But I reckon I never was so well paid before."

CHAPTER
TWENTY

The Race for Range

Monday morning dawned bright and clear, as do so many days in Nevada. Cattlemen and herder were ready for the run. The cattlemen were moving toward the Reserve from half a dozen points.

Cantrell spoke of armed resistance and saw that his men carried their guns. At the Lazy K he was taken seriously. Wheeler, Adams — all the others — were uncommunicative. They were ready for trouble. The Basques had best be careful.

Big Jim recognized, if they did not, that this was not their original attitude. They had passed from the offensive to the defensive. Well, they could do as they pleased; he would do the same.

He spoke to Bridger. Chris echoed his sentiments, but not as he once had. He wanted to know about Thane's sheep. Cantrell told him not to worry on that score.

Shortly after dawn the run began. The line of the Reserve was passed without trouble occurring anywhere. Once in the National Forest, the trails began to converge. Soon sheep were flowing along side by side with the cattle. The best grazing was at the headwaters of Martins Creek. Naturally it was the common goal. All of the big outfits had sent their herds in. Each man was out for himself this day.

The cattle moved faster than the sheep, but there were ten sheep to every steer. The Basques were heavily armed, which was not usually the case. They were out in force, too, glum and watchful.

Cantrell rode at the head of his men. The Basques did not get out of his way. They carried rifles in the crooks of their arms, and they were cocked.

A bunch of Double A steers got in the path of the Lazy K herd. Cantrell ordered Uncle Henry to drive through them. In a minute there was a pitched battle. Fists flew and blood flowed. The Lazy K won out. Adams' men soon drew reinforcements, however, and found allies to stand with them.

It was only an instance of what was occurring everywhere. Irquieaga had come to blows with Bridger's foreman. Shots had been fired, but no one was wounded.

Irquieaga and Cantrell came face to face before the morning was half gone. The Basque rode a great white stallion. He had licked Bridger's man and was spoiling to mix it with Cantrell.

"Well, what you theenk now, eh? I guess you see we here. Why don' you do something about eet?" he taunted.

"I'll take care of you when I ain't so busy," Cantrell growled.

"You was never too busy before! Eet was you I see crawl out of the cañon yesterday. You set fire to eet."

192

"Did I?" Jim answered insolently.

"Lots of good it deed you. T'ane's flock don't get touched."

"The hell it didn't! Where are his sheep?"

"That's Esteban over there by those beeg flat. I guess you see heem all right eef you look."

Cantrell's rage could not be measured by words. Aaron Thane's flock was on the Reserve and here was this bullying Basque making him take water.

But he wouldn't admit defeat. He'd find a way even yet for driving Aaron out. As for Irquieaga, he'd meet him sometime when he didn't have a hundred of his countrymen to back him up.

The strife continued all day. It became apparent to the more level-headed ones that some sane method of apportioning the range must be found.

"Angel Irosabal is the only man who can bring order out of this mess," Wheeler declared to Adams and Bridger and one or two others. "He is not in the Reserve. God knows what will happen overnight, but we'll see Angel in the morning. I'll send word that we're coming."

They agreed to this.

"It will be give and take," Wheeler went on. "Tell your men to be careful until we get back."

Del Ryan brought Cantrell word of this meeting that evening. "Why didn't they ask you?" he demanded to know. "Bridger has been invited to set in. I thought you had been made the leader."

"What, me crawl to that old bosko? Not on your life! I'll fight 'em to the finish!"

Cantrell tried desperately to save his face.

"You've made a botch of everything," Del stormed. "I suspected from the first that this charge against Kincaid and McCarroll was a frame-up. They've caught the real thief now, thanks to McCarroll. You're going to have some explaining to do if this man Dolores talks, and he will, undoubtedly."

Cantrell could not successfully dissemble his chagrin at this startling news. It not only made him furious but increased his resentment against Kincaid and Flash, if that were possible.

"Stuff like that don't get you anything," Del summed up after acquainting Cantrell with such details of Dolores' arrest as he knew. "Even Bridger seems to have turned against you."

"Well, he don't want to try any funny work on me," Jim threatened. "I've got enough on him to make him be good."

Del was only mildly interested in this.

"It's hell to think that we've got good range that's at its best now and have to leave it for grass we're paying for. Two months from now what will be left in the Reserve? We'll bring our cattle home to the burnt up stuff that's good now. We lose both ways. We should have made some arrangement with the Basques to parcel out the Reserve."

"You're pretty late with that idea," Cantrell sneered. "You didn't talk that way this spring."

That this was true did not improve Del's temper.

"I didn't say it because I was listening to you," he shot back. "Why did you have to lose your head over

194

that Thane girl? You had to go out to *get* Kincaid just because he was shining up to her. He was good enough for you until she showed up."

"Don't you go too far," Cantrell threatened.

"I've had my say," Del retorted. "My money is invested here; don't forget that. You see me before you make any more fool plays."

Wheeler and Angel Irosabal reached an understanding the following morning.

Cantrell's answer was to get fiendishly drunk for two days. On the second night after Del's visit he stole into the Reserve and left a red trail behind him. He escaped unseen and was so impressed with his success that he returned the following night.

In the meantime, Kincaid had seen nothing of Frazier. He made it a habit to go into the Reserve every evening. He had met Aaron once. Esteban had reported the killing of more sheep. The old man appealed to the rangers for protection, but they refused to become involved. They argued that if anyone were caught violating the law he would be arrested, but they refused to constitute themselves guardians of any man's flock.

Lin had anticipated this stand and he was not surprised to learn that the almost nightly slaughter continued. Flash's continued absence had begun to worry him sorely.

The effect of this guerrilla warfare was apparent on Aaron. This nightly killing of his sheep could mean only complete disaster eventually.

Lin suspected that it was only Aaron's pride that kept his head up now. He feared that conditions would grow worse, for he knew that Cantrell would not be content to wait for this patient game of bushwacking to drive the Thanes out. But that Cantrell could hope for any greater success now was almost beyond belief.

By mistake the following night, Cantrell got into Irquieaga's flock. The big Basque caught him almost red-handed. He was armed with cause for retaliation now, and he proceeded to make the most of it. Two nights later the Lazy K ranch-house burned to the ground. Cantrell was put to no great effort to surmise who was responsible.

Del came once more. He had heard of the raids on the flocks in the Reserve. He accused Cantrell of being guilty. Big Jim denied vehemently that he was responsible.

"One more misstep and we part company," Ryan warned before he left.

For a week following the fire nothing happened of note. Kincaid saw Frazier for a moment. He did not share her belief that Cantrell had learned his lesson.

Several nights later he saw Cantrell ride up to Parr's shack.

An overwhelming desire to learn what business he had there caused him to make his way down to the place.

The night was cool, but Newt had not closed the windows. Their talk was all of Aaron Thane. Cantrell convicted himself in a sentence of the nightly killings. He swore that he was tired of trying to drive Aaron out that way.

"Thane's got five or six thousand in the bank. We've got to unload this mine on him. If I get him strapped

196

he'll sell his ranch at my price. He's sick of sheep already. Mighty sick, I take it. We can dress up this mine so she'll pass an assay test — salt her, I mean. Those assayers down in Winnemucca say you've got the same sort of quartz here that Starr is takin' a fortune out of at the Big Ben. I can buy enough high grade from him to make this place look pretty."

Newt scratched his head reflectively.

"Men go to jail for that sort of thing, Jim," he said.

"Humph!" Cantrell snorted. "You don't think Thane is suspicious of you?"

"Not him; but that girl of his ain't no fool. How much money can we get out of him?"

Cantrell laughed loudly.

"So it's the price that's worryin' you, eh? Sell him just a half interest. That'll sound more plausible. He'd wonder about you lettin' go of all of it if it's as valuable as you're goin' to make him believe."

He got up and paced the floor as he went over the details of this latest scheme.

"This thing's all right," he announced at last. "You're selling a half interest because you need money to work the property. Don't urge him; don't be too anxious. Give him a little time and he'll drop like a duck in a pond."

"I haven't heard you say yet how we are to split what we get," Newt said pointedly.

"We'll split it even. Does that satisfy you?"

"I reckon it does. You'll have to do the arranging with Starr and bring the stuff here. I haven't any way of getting it."

"Certainly! I'll bring it in to-morrow night. Early the next mornin' you beat it for town. Go by the Thane place. Be sure they see you. Don't tell him anythin'; just be mysterious with him. That'll get him sure."

They spent another hour perfecting their plans before Cantrell got up to leave. Newt came to the door with him.

"Jim," he declared solemnly as Cantrell got into his saddle, "don't you double-cross me like you did Kincaid and McCarroll. Prison wouldn't appeal to me. I reckon I'd kill you before I got took."

His cold scrutiny forced Big Jim to answer.

"Talk like that won't git you nothin'," he muttered angrily. "You keep your mouth shut and we won't have any trouble."

Kincaid's first thought was to warn Aaron. Morning found him of a different mind. All the cards were in his hands now, and for the first time he felt sure that he could square his score with Cantrell.

The mine was "salted" that night. In the early hours of the following morning Newt dashed away from Emigrant Creek.

He rode at such a wild pace that his horse was soon covered with lather. For years he had dreamed of galloping to town in this fashion with the news that he had found a fortune. Unconsciously he began to accept make-believe for reality.

That perverse fate which watches over the destinies of some must have smiled at the dénouement that followed.

Aaron had been about to ride away for the Reserve when Frazier caught sight of the rapidly moving dust-cloud approaching from the southwest.

It moved so swiftly that it could betoken only danger or excitement of some sort. This feeling grew on them as they waited, and when Aaron recognized Newt Parr he leaped to the conclusion that something of importance had transpired on Emigrant Creek.

Newt pretended not to see them as he dashed toward the house, flailing his poor horse with his arms and knees.

Aaron called to him. He looked up, then.

"No time to stop," he shouted back. "I'm rich! *Rich*, do you hear?"

Newt seemed to be truly mad. For all his excitement, he had slowed his horse down. He acted now as if it had been a waste of precious seconds and began to kick and pummel the brute again.

"What is it, man?" Aaron cried, almost as excited as Newt now. "Is it your mine?"

"Mine? Of course! I've struck a fortune, I tell you. I've got to get to town right away."

"Why do you want to do that? Why blab this news up and down the land and have an army rushing here to beat you out of what you've found?"

Newt wheeled his horse about with indecision.

"There is some sense in that," he groaned as he mopped his face. His old jaws worked convulsively and his eyes were wild looking.

Frazier pitied him.

Shrewd old fraud that he was, he capitulated slowly. In the end the three rode back to Emigrant Creek.

Lin, from his perch above Newt's shack, saw them arrive. It was the middle of the afternoon before they left. That night he rode to the ranch.

A glance at Aaron was enough to tell him that the deadly virus of that madness called Gold had conquered him. He was younger-looking, plainly refreshed and running over with confidence.

Lin shook his head pityingly. He had seen this happen to other men.

"There's no reason for your distrust of Newt Parr," Aaron dared to say in answer to Lin's quiet skepticism. "You've proven yourself a good friend, Lin, but don't forget that you accuse a man you are unwilling to face."

"You know why I don't want to meet him," Lin answered stiffly.

"Oh, Father," Frazier hurried to say, "don't misunderstand Lin."

"It's his fault," Old Aaron replied. "I will not listen to any more wild talk about Newt Parr."

"You won't hear any from me," Lin assured him, his patience at an end. He turned to go. Frazier followed him to the door. "When they drive to town to-morrow to have the assays made," said he, "you insist on your father gettin' an engineer to look over the property before he signs any papers. An assay doesn't prove anythin' if a mine has been salted."

"I promise you I will," she murmured. "You are not angry, Lin?"

200

"I'll get over it if I am," he answered in better humor. "You know there is nothin' I wouldn't do for you folks. I don't want to see you tricked out of all you own. You run in now, and don't have any words on my account. Take my word for it, somethin's goin' to happen to Mr. Newt Parr."

CHAPTER
TWENTY-ONE

Empty Pockets

Kincaid's parting words were prompted by something most definite, or he would have told Frazier what he had overheard between Newt and Cantrell. He had gone to the Thanes to suggest a line of action, but Aaron's attitude had driven him away.

Resentment still rankled in him. He had so seldom worried about other people or gone out of his way to fight for them that he couldn't understand old Aaron's seeming ingratitude.

Proud, sensitive to a degree one would have hardly expected, he was to be forgiven for sulking.

Morning found him quite himself again and of a mind to do as he had first planned.

He saw Aaron come for Newt. Half an hour later they drove away in Aaron's buggy. He knew it would be night, or even early morning before they returned. If Frazier succeeded in making her father engage an engineer to inspect Newt's property they would hardly be back before the following evening. In any event, Kincaid knew they would be out of the way long enough to suit his plans.

Lin was not foolish enough to suppose that their going removed all chance of failure for him, for Cantrell remained to be reckoned with. He sat in his doorway, cleaning his guns and calculating his chances of success.

He took to the hills, finally, and scoured the cañon from end to end. Far across the open desert he could see the small cloud of dust that Aaron's horse kicked up as it loped along.

Nothing else moved in the wide waste. Lin decided to take the chance that he was alone on the creek. Cantrell and he would have to settle things some day, anyhow. If it fell that this was to be the day, he was ready.

Having come to a decision, he lost no time in reaching the mine. All morning he toiled there, lowering himself into the tunnel by way of the orebucket and getting back to the surface when necessary by hand-over-hand climbing of the rope that was fastened to the windlass.

In the course of three hours he had made the round-trip ten or eleven times, always bringing to the surface part of the precious ore with which Cantrell and Newt had "salted" the drift.

No one came to stop him. Lin spent many minutes searching the distant hills and rimrocks. Raucous-tongued magpies sailed lazily in the sky — proof enough that no one moved below them.

By noontime the last of the high grade had been brought to the surface. To the unpracticed eye the drift in which Newt had made his alleged discovery remained as it had been.

Kincaid ventured a smile as he took a last look about. If any values remained they were the ones nature had placed there.

He obliterated his tracks. All that he had to do now was to hide the rich quartz. The choosing of the spot in which to conceal it revealed diabolic ingenuity of such a high order that Lin was unable to control his mirth for a moment.

The tunnel of his own abandoned mine was the place he selected. What a grim joke that was!

"Even Cantrell ought to laugh at that," he drawled.

It took him as long to erase his trail up the cañon as it did to transfer the ore. An additional hour spent in turning over the tailings of his old mine completed his work. He was ready for Cantrell's next move.

His patience received a severe test, however, as he waited.

Big Jim made himself conspicuous in Paradise that day, being accompanied by a bodyguard of his own men. It was the finest sort of an alibi. The mine on Emigrant Creek might never have existed, for all his apparent concern.

Frazier had won her point with her father, and when Aaron and Newt reached Paradise on the way back from Winnemucca, Cantrell's face fell as he saw that Ry Blodgett, the mining engineer, rode with them.

With morning came the calamity!

"Nothing — absolutely nothing — here," Blodgett told Newt and Aaron. "If those samples came out of this drift you must have tapped a little, pinched-out stringer."

Newt's hand trembled violently as he searched for a piece of the high grade and found none.

"But those samples were rich," he gasped, utterly bewildered. "I couldn't have taken out the whole stringer."

He picked up piece after piece of rock from the floor of the drift. Despair began to grip him. He was a miner, he did not have to pass over the pieces he fingered to Blodgett; they were valueless.

His old eyes searched the drift carefully. His heart sank, then. The mine looked as they had left it; but it was not. Someone had "dusted" it!

He wanted to cry out "Thief!" He ran to the windlass to look for signs, but realized all too soon that they themselves had destroyed any evidence the thieves might have left.

Parr knew he had talked a lot in town. Someone might have dashed here from Paradise on a tip by telephone from Winnemucca.

Or was Cantrell's fine hand in this? He was willing to believe anything in his despair. He gasped as though something was smothering him and driving him mad.

He no longer cared what Aaron thought; Aaron was a fool and a dupe. But Blodgett was no tyro.

Newt knew that the engineer was eyeing him suspiciously. With unseeing eyes, he stumbled away, muttering miserably to himself, "I can't stand it, I can't stand it."

Aaron and Blodgett completely misunderstood his emotion, seeing before them only an old broken man who had let his enthusiasm run away with his judgment.

Newt realized what they failed to grasp. Not only was this present enterprise a failure, but any future sale of the mine was beyond the realm of possibility now, for Blodgett had damned it. Gold might be there at lower levels, but who would pay for the chance of finding it? He knew miners. All that remained to him was a hole in the ground.

Aaron was almost as downcast and morose. This mine had opened up wonderful vistas to him. He had seen himself as he wanted to be — a rich, picturesque Westerner — a booster of Nevada's untouched resources, a philanthropist who would send the story of the state's greatness ringing up and down the world.

Blodgett's dashing of their hopes awakened no mistrust of Newt in his mind. He, at least, could go back to his sheep. What was Newt to do? "Better go home with me," he said miserably. "I can't leave you here alone."

Parr was unmoved by this solicitude. There was nothing he wanted so much as to be alone just then. So there they left him to give vent to his long-pent-up agony.

Cantrell came at nightfall and delivered himself of a torrent of words on learning what had happened. But once satisfied that the mine had been stripped, he lost no time in lamentation.

"Sellin' the mine wasn't anythin' more than a way of gettin' rid of old Thane," he declared. "I'm out what the ore cost, that's all."

"That's all you're out," Newt groaned. "What about me?"

"Well, what about you? I've been shellin' out pretty regular to you for years. What I want to know is — who did this? Everyone in town last night knew your business. Time you git to be two or three hundred years old you'll savvy the sense of keepin' your mouth shut."

"Don't you pick on me too hard," Newt warned him.

"Don't pick on yuh? You stay here and keep still. I'll find out somethin' about this."

Newt did not retort. Cantrell was miles away before he even moved. He saw how little he figured in Cantrell's plans. The failure of their scheme was only a setback to Cantrell — something that to-morrow could right.

It was not that way with him. He was left high and dry, his days of scheming at an end.

"Just a useless old bag of bones," he muttered as he drank the dregs of failure. He pondered over his own words, for he jumped to his feet a few minutes later and answered himself. "Ain't neither!" he exclaimed shrilly. "I reckon there's something left, 'way down under the rust."

He knocked the ashes from his pipe and marched to the door.

"Hey, you, Daisy!" he called to his horse, "me and you are going to travel. You stay nigh till I'm ready."

He had looked up and down Emigrant Creek ten thousand times in his days on the creek, and the impulse to do so now was strong, but he resisted it.

"Reckon it ain't changed none," he muttered. "Been lookin' at it too long as it is."

An hour later he had his pack ready. With the lead rope in his hand he and Daisy headed for the West. He had no destination in mind. Some distant ridge or cañon would claim them. So it was that he passed from Emigrant Creek as he had come to it — older, but no richer.

CHAPTER
TWENTY-TWO

Face to Face

Frazier Thane knew before her father had spoken a word that Newt Parr's mine had proved a disappointment. She curbed her curiosity, however, and waited for him to speak. His story did not concern Kincaid; but Frazier drew her own conclusions. It was plain enough to her that Lin had saved them a second time.

All her tactfulness was needed to restore her father's faith in himself. She did not mention Lin's name, fearing he might sense some unintended slap at Newt.

They had neither seen nor heard from Esteban in three days. No news was good news, however, and Frazier finally saw her father taking heart again.

Kincaid had left the dugout in the meantime, realizing that Cantrell would certainly make some effort to trace the missing high grade. Lin's mine was only a hundred yards below the dugout. Twelve feet above the mine dump a shelving ledge cut back into the cañon wall for a few feet. He moved there with his blanket and some canned stuff after turning Piñon lose in the basin.

From this perch he could command a view up and down the cañon for several miles. But nothing happened the first day to disturb the tranquillity of Emigrant Creek.

Kincaid's thoughts turned to Frazier.

Thinking of her left him unhappy, his life a series of regrets. Undoubtedly the chief cause of his dissatisfaction with himself — a fact which quite escaped him — was that he never before had indulged in introspection of this sort.

The following morning he was relieved to see a man coming up the cañon. The newcomer's movements were calculated to arouse his instant suspicion. He was on foot. He picked his way up the creek very carefully, staying close to the wall and traveling over the malpais and rock falls.

Lin saw him stop at Parr's shack. He came out presently and looked up and down the cañon excitedly. Kincaid did not know that Newt had left the creek. That the man below him had come expecting to see Parr was evident.

Lin strained his eyes in an effort to recognize the stranger, who was continuing up the creek, now. He kept to the rocks and avoided the easier way of the trail. Lin understood that stepping from rock to rock; this stranger was not leaving any trail. By now Kincaid saw that the man carried a rifle.

A projecting ledge hid him from view for a few minutes. When he reappeared, Kincaid recognized him. The man was Cantrell.

Lin covered him as he came nearer and nearer. A twitch of the finger and Big Jim's hulking body would have crashed to earth.

No least suspicion of Lin's presence entered Cantrell's mind. His one concern seemed to be behind him, for he continually stopped to gaze down the cañon.

A small, moving speck coming up the lower creek caught Kincaid's eye. Evidently it was for this that Cantrell watched.

Big Jim was so near now that Lin could hear him muttering angrily to himself. Lin's hatred of the man almost got the better of him, and the impulse to stand up and shoot it out with Cantrell was not easily conquered.

Cantrell did not stop at Lin's cabin but came on directly to the mine. Watcher and watched were only twelve feet apart.

Every move that Cantrell made — the raising of the sights on his rifle, the pumping of a shell into the barrel, the training of the gun on the figure coming up the creek — were seen by Lin. It was murder, cold and deliberate.

"Newt Parr!" Kincaid whispered to himself. "They've had a fallin' out and now he's goin' to bump him off."

What else was he to think? But why did Cantrell come here to pick him off? Why hadn't he stayed at the shack?

That they had fallen out over the fiasco at the mine was most likely. Newt had stopped but a moment at his shack. He would hardly be off his guard.

Lin noticed that he rode boldly up the trail as though defying Cantrell.

A minute later Big Jim's rifle went to his shoulder. Suddenly Lin's mouth sagged as he stared at the man on horseback. This was not Newt Parr.

It was Aaron Thane!

Lin did not wait to use his gun, but gathered himself together like a panther and leaped through the air. He landed squarely upon Cantrell, knocking the breath out of him.

Kincaid's head swam from the force with which he landed. Cantrell had not moved. To all appearances he was dead. Blood flowed from a nasty cut across his temple.

Lin groped about for the cowman's gun, but it was gone, knocked out of his hands. Satisfied of this, Kincaid sank back, anxious to have Aaron pass without knowing they were there. If Cantrell lived, certain things would be settled immediately, matters which did not concern Aaron.

The previous day had been a bad one for Cantrell. Del Ryan had arrived at the Lazy K with word that Joe Dolores was going to trial in Elko that morning. Del still fumed about the fire which had destroyed the ranch buildings. Cantrell unwisely tried to defend himself, with the result that Del had threatened to sell out. Before he left he practically placed Uncle Henry, the Lazy K foreman, in charge of the ranch.

The effect of all this on Cantrell need hardly be stated. Liquor did not dispel the growing conviction that he was licked. Defeat made a mad dog of him. Aaron became the living symbol of all those who had defied him. From that moment he had had no other purpose than to slay the man.

Kincaid knew nothing of all this. Aaron had passed into the basin before he was able to stand and see clearly. Cantrell still lay inert, but Lin knew that he lived. He was in no hurry to have him sit up. He had waited so long to square accounts with Big Jim that a few minutes now could not matter.

What his feelings were as he gazed upon the white face of the man who had put a price on him can be imagined.

Cantrell moved slightly. Kincaid tossed away his guns. Both were unarmed now. This was the way he had always wanted to settle matters with him.

The big man opened his eyes a few seconds later. A film still fogged them. He gazed dumbly at Lin, not recognizing him at first.

"You — Kincaid!" he muttered at last.

Lin nodded. "Don't bother lookin' for your rifle," he said. "It won't take any guns to settle this."

Cantrell stared at him for a long while before he summoned a grin to his battered face. "Still a kid, ain't you?" he leered. "You'll learn!"

Lin did not reply. His silence emboldened Cantrell to a further taunt. "Jumped me from that ledge, eh?" he went on. "We could have finished this without any grand-standin'."

And still Lin said nothin. It began to exasperate Cantrell.

"Too bad you couldn't 'a' waited until I'd finished that old fool," he snarled. "Suppose you think you've got it on me forty ways now. We got it on each other, so to speak, ain't we?"

"You have your fun, Cantrell," Lin whipped out. "It'll be some time before you enjoy yourself again."

"Yeh? Shows how old-fashioned I'm gettin', never suspectin' that you'd be hidin' out so close by. I suppose your friend McCarroll is round-abouts, too."

"I wish he were," Lin drawled. "I'd like to have him see what I'm goin' to do to you."

Cantrell held his tongue, so cold and searching did he find Kincaid's gaze.

"What I'm goin' to do, I'll do with these," Lin drove on, holding up his hands. "You let me know when you feel able to get up."

Cantrell could and would fight. But he wondered what Kincaid knew about the developments over in Elko. With this in mind he said craftily:

"That's pretty hostile talk for a man who's wanted himself."

"You know why I'm wanted," Lin flung at him. "I'm goin' back to Elko, and you're goin' with me, Cantrell!"

Jim was not convinced of that, even if he was that Lin knew nothing about Dolores. This success tempted him to find out if Kincaid knew about the salting of Parr's mine.

Lin suspected his purpose before he had said a dozen words. It pleased him to let Cantrell believe he had been looking after Aaron's sheep.

"You didn't stop at nothin' when you fell did yuh?" Cantrell leered at him. "I didn't think you'd git that low. Anythin' to get the girl, eh?"

214

"Get up!" Lin ground out at that.

Cantrell leaped to his feet and came at him, hunched over, his eyes flaming with hate.

Lin did not back away, but shot a blow to Big Jim's jaw. Cantrell took it for all it was worth. If this was Kincaid's best, he had nothing to fear.

They circled around and around, then, Cantrell content to wait and Lin seeking an opening. Suddenly Cantrell thought he saw his chance. He sent a smashing hook to Lin's heart, but Lin got out of the way in time. A second later Cantrell tried it again, but once more Lin stepped out of danger. This time, however, Jim hung on to him. Kincaid rained blows on his face; but Cantrell smothered them and continued to hang on, forcing Lin to drag him back and forth.

Cantrell wasn't fighting. He was waiting and wearing down the smaller man. Lin sensed his intention and fumed at himself for ever allowing the fighting to get to close quarters.

Already Cantrell's face was cut badly. And yet, Lin knew that unless he dislodged the weight about his neck he fought a losing battle.

He stepped backward without warning. With rifle-like quickness Lin drove a crushing blow into the big man's stomach. Cantrell winced. Another jab followed. Again he grunted. He couldn't stand these body blows. He loosened his hold on Kincaid and sent him reeling backward with his knee.

Lin strove to catch himself as he saw Cantrell brace to kick. He could not escape it, but managed to catch

Cantrell's boot and twist the big fellow's leg. They fell together with a thud.

They got to their feet warily. Lin bore no marks of the struggle, but of the two he was the more tired. As they came together again he did his best to keep out of the embrace of those big arms.

He feinted with his left to draw up Cantrell's guard. It was successful once or twice and he sent crashing blows to the body. Lin's spirit soared every time he landed, even though he knew his strength was going. It but proved again the wisdom of that wise old saw to the effect that a good little man can never beat a fairly good big man. The endurance is not there.

Cantrell had come to the battle whipped mentally. That feeling was gone now. Optimism made him bold; he would be on his feet when Kincaid was no longer able to lift his hands.

"I told you you'd learn, you baby," Cantrell mocked. "Why don't you fight?"

For a time he became the aggressor. Lin let Jim chase him around. Suddenly Cantrell whirled and his arms caught Kincaid and drew him in.

The big man hugged him until their faces rubbed and Lin's was smeared with blood. He remembered Cantrell's trick with the knee. He raised his and sent it deep into the pit of the man's stomach.

Cantrell drew back in pain and his arms fell. Lin's fist was not more than eighteen inches from the other's jaw. It was not far for a blow to travel, but into it he put his very soul — a crashing, bone-breaking uppercut.

It caught Cantrell on the point of the jaw. Another moment and he crumpled to the ground unconscious.

Kincaid stood over him swaying crazily, repaid in part for what he had suffered at Cantrell's hands. A child could have pushed him over, he was so weak.

Once he fancied he felt a sustaining arm about his waist. A trick of the imagination, he told himself.

But no! Someone was speaking to him.

"Oh, it was wonderful, Lin!"

He raised his head slowly and turned his blinking eyes upon this strange phantom that was not a phantom after all. Recognition dawned in his eyes.

"Frazier!" he mumbled incredulously, refusing to believe his eyes.

"Yes, Lin, I've been here for almost five minutes."

He felt ashamed that she had witnessed what had taken place.

"Disgusting?" she cried in answer. "Why, it was perfectly thrilling. Cantrell deserved all that you gave him."

CHAPTER
TWENTY-THREE

McCarroll Comes Home

Frazier had watched her father as he left that morning until he had disappeared in the first low hills that swelled away to Emigrant Creek. She had returned to her household duties then, but as the minutes passed she had become obsessed with a presentiment of danger.

She was level-headed, as a rule, but fear of the unknown thing that tugged at her consciousness finally drove her out of the house. Then, in an attempt to overtake Aaron, she had raced to the creek.

She soon knew how well grounded her fear had been. With a punishing effort she managed to keep the tears back on learning what Cantrell had attempted.

"I'll repay you for this some day, Lin," she whispered, knowing how well he had served her.

"If you mean that, ma'am, get your father to sell out. This is no game for him. It won't be quittin'; it'll just be recognizin' the fact that you can't play it square and win against such skunks as this."

"Even if I could make him see that, it would be difficult to find a buyer, I think," she answered.

Frazier finally promised to speak to her father.

It was five minutes later that Cantrell sat up and stared at them vacantly. Kincaid appeared to pay no attention to him. No trace of guile crept into Kincaid's voice as he talked on, but his words were pointed for Cantrell's ears now.

"Are you able to ride to town?" he asked Frazier. "You'll be safe with my horse."

He was so deadly serious of a sudden that Frazier glanced at him apprehensively.

"Why, yes," said she. "What is it, Lin?"

"I want you to go to the recorder's office and file on the claims above and below this one. I'll give you some money to pay up the back assessments on the old claim."

Frazier stared at him in amazement.

"Lin Kincaid," she exclaimed, "what are you trying to say?"

This talk of filing claims interested Cantrell, too. He had no doubt but what it was Lin who had "dusted" Parr's mine.

"Just this," Lin lied with consummate art, "my days of workin' for wages are over. While I've been hidin' out here I amused myself by pokin' into the old mine. I've found somethin' good."

"And you've kept this to yourself for days?" Frazier demanded excitedly.

"Thought you'd been herdin' sheep," Cantrell cut in sarcastically.

"I've been herdin' 'em right here," Lin answered him. Turning to Frazier he said: "What could I have done? I'd been locked up if I showed my face in town.

My days of hidin' out are over now. When you get back, Cantrell and I are goin' to take a little trip. If you'll notice, I've put up the monuments on these three claims already. File on the lower one for yourself. I want you to have it."

"That's pritty crude," Cantrell muttered. "I reckon I know where you got the stuff you claim to have found."

Lin ignored this shot. He was busily telling Frazier what to do.

"Above all, ma'am," he begged, "don't talk when you get to town. I don't want any army campin' here by night. That'll happen if this gets out."

"Are you sure, Lin?" she queried. "Have you really found something?"

"Wait!"

He went into the tunnel. When he came out he carried several pieces of the high grade he had taken out of Parr's mine. By design he let one piece fall so that Cantrell could retrieve it.

"Take these with you, Frazier," he said. "You might ask Blodgett what he thinks of 'em."

Cantrell picked up the piece of quartz and examined it carefully. He saw unmistakable values in it. It looked exactly like the ore he had bought for Parr. But how could he be certain? Kincaid's talk of secrecy had piqued his interest. Unbidden, he got up to investigate the tunnel.

Lin whirled on him. "Get back!" he cried. "You sit down. I'll tell you when to move."

Cantrell obeyed. Although his body was battered, his eyes glittered with something of their old fire.

220

Covetousness was in them — greed. A man didn't spend money paying up old assessments and filing fees where as little was involved as the value of the ore taken from Parr's drift.

Lin found his guns and Cantrell's. Leaving Frazier at the mine, he and Big Jim went to the basin and caught Piñon. They were back promptly.

"Don't worry about him," Lin assured her, nodding at Cantrell. "We'll wait here until you get back. Your father will be passin' on his way out. I'll tell him where you have gone."

Frazier's genuine excitement did as much as anything else to make Cantrell believe that Kincaid might really have struck it. Strike or not, he wanted to get into action, to find out what the tunnel held. He turned away as Frazier headed Piñon down the cañon. For a wonder, he had no desire to hear her good-bye to Kincaid.

Time passed slowly after she left. Lin had nothing to say to Cantrell. At last Big Jim spoke to him.

"I never appreciated you, Kincaid," said he. "You're cleverer than I thought you was. You ain't got anythin' here and you know it."

Lin laughed at him, and his amusement was not all feigned, for he sensed that Cantrell's curiosity and credulity were overcoming his better judgment.

"What I've got here don't interest you," he snapped. "You remember that, Cantrell."

"If you have got somethin'," Cantrell came back, "why be foolish? Maybe I could square that trouble over in Elko."

"You couldn't square anythin' for me," Lin replied as he turned away to hide his satisfaction.

"No? Say, about two hundred dollars' worth of high grade disappeared from Parr's mine lately. I aim to find it."

"Why don't you ask Newt what became of it," Lin replied nonchalantly.

The shot reached home. Here was a field for speculation that Cantrell had overlooked. He knew Newt was capable of such a trick. Conversation died as the big fellow mused over this.

Shortly before noon, Lin heard voices in the cañon above.

"This will be Aaron," he told himself. A few minutes later he recognized the old man. There was something familiar about the man who rode with him. Lin got to his feet and scrutinized him closely.

"Flash, or I'm blind!" he exclaimed aloud, forgetting Cantrell.

Big Jim turned and studied the approaching men. He saw that Lin was right.

"Come down out of your hole, you old tumbleweed," Flash shouted a moment later.

Lin waved him up to the mine. They clasped hands warmly. There was nothing to say how glad they were to see each other again.

"And here is little Jimmy," Flash chuckled. "What's happened to you, baby?"

Cantrell snarled at him and turned away.

"Why did I have to miss this?" McCarroll wailed. "Always too late: that's me."

222

Aaron demanded an explanation, too. Lin obliged.

"Let me finish him," Flash begged. "If your conscience hurts you, you can go down the cañon for a few minutes."

McCarroll had met Aaron by accident in the Reserve. He was on his way to the cabin at the time with news of what had happened in Elko the past morning. Dolores had not talked. He had taken his ten years without mentioning Cantrell's name.

"But you'll be on the inside lookin' out anyhow, Cantrell," said Flash. "That prosecutin' attorney ain't no fool. They'll be after you in a day or two; and Del Ryan won't stop 'em."

"How do we stand?" Lin asked.

"O.K. Not even an assault charge against us for bangin' up your friend with the jug."

"Great!" Lin exclaimed. "We're not only free, but rich!"

"What?"

"You wait!" Lin admonished him.

They drew apart and left Aaron to watch Cantrell. Lin listened as Flash related how he had trailed Dolores and finally trapped him. Lin had much to tell also. He spoke of the mine last.

"And you've really got it?" Flash exclaimed.

"Not a thing," said Lin. "This is all put on for Cantrell's benefit. Frazier has promised to get her father to sell out. I'm goin' to provide the buyer. That'll be Cantrell. This mine will be the bait. You play it with me, Flash, and see how close I come to makin' good. I'm goin' to let you ride herd on Cantrell. About one o'clock you manage to let him get away. Verne Remmington, the head ranger, has a telephone at his cabin. Cantrell will use it. He'll get in touch with Del or someone in Paradise. The news will spread. Don't be surprised if there's a mob campin' out here to-night. I'll get the old man out of the way in a few minutes."

They returned to the dump and entered the tunnel without glancing at Cantrell. A moment later Flash's cry of astonishment brought both Aaron and the big fellow to their feet.

"Whew!" Flash exclaimed as they came out. "No more punchin' cattle for you, old-timer."

"Nor for you!" Lin declared. "This claim above mine is yours. Miss Frazier is in town filin' for me now."

What was all this talk of mines and claims? Had everyone gone crazy? Aaron looked the astonishment he could not voice.

"Go into the tunnel and have a look," Lin advised him.

"My, my, Lin," he exclaimed as he rejoined them, "how could you keep this a secret? I was interested in Parr's mine, but it never looked as promising as this. I'm going to stake out a claim right away. There must be gold in great quantities on this creek. Fortunes will be made here yet."

Lin told him that the claim below his own was to belong to Frazier. "Stake out another one while there's time, if you care to."

Aaron thought that he would; two chances were always better than one.

224

"I'll file to-morrow," said he when he came back from building one of those strange little monuments which the law recognizes as first proof of possession.

"I hope that will be soon enough," Lin murmured with a thought for Cantrell. "You know how these things break sometimes."

The fever of all this got into Cantrell's blood. He was no longer the scoffer.

"How about me?" he dared to ask.

"Well, how about yuh?" Lin drawled. "You don't figure in this at all."

He started to say something else as Lin and Aaron left for the dugout.

"What's the matter, can't you understand when a gentleman speaks to you?" Flash demanded. "Sit down and shut up! I'm givin' orders now."

Cantrell was in for a sorry hour. Every time he as much as glanced at him McCarroll lashed him with his tongue. When he began to feign sleep it was like a cat playing with a mouse. He would let Cantrell reach the edge of the dump, when an imaginary fly or insect of some sort would appear to have lighted upon the McCarroll face. Flash would sit up and glare angrily. Cantrell would crawl back to his place. Once he almost succeeded in leaping from the tailings.

"I'll make an angel out of yuh, if I catch you doin' that again," Flash railed at him. "I'm a horse-thief, eh? Say, why don't you jump? I'll get you on the wing."

It was about the best fun Flash had had in many months. He was sorry to see one o'clock arrive. Cantrell waited until it seemed McCarroll's snoring would awaken him in itself, so violent was it. He was fifty yards away and running rapidly when Flash thought it safe to open his eyes.

Lin had seen Cantrell go. He came to the mine to call McCarroll.

"I see he's gone," said he.

"Gone?" Flash cried. "Say, he'd have got away even if we'd wanted to keep him, he was that anxious!"

CHAPTER
TWENTY-FOUR

Lady Luck

Cantrell worked quickly. Frazier had not yet left the recorder's office when a man dashed into the room and engaged that official in an excited aside. Frazier heard Emigrant Creek mentioned. By the time she reached the street the news had spread like prairie fire. Was it true Kincaid had found a bonanza? Where were his claims located? When was the strike made?

She saw men and women preparing to leave immediately for the creek. She passed the barbershop. A hastily scrawled sign hung on the closed door. "Gone to Emigrant Creek!" it read.

Only the Basques seemed undisturbed by the news that Cantrell had telephoned to Ike Leonard, one of Ryan's lieutenants, with a strict promise of secrecy, but which was already public property.

Down in Winnemucca Del had been reached. He had close friends who had to be told, too. The effect there was quite the same as in Paradise. An old Ford whirled down Bridge Street, headed for Paradise. Hill. In the space of half an hour a dozen others followed it.

This thing gathered momentum with every passing minute. Nevada has witnessed a hundred similar "rushes" that had nothing more tangible than this to set them in motion.

The scene which met Frazier's eyes when she rode out of Paradise less than hour later filled her with chagrin. Lin had wanted no one to know about his find. Now, apparently, everyone knew. How had the news leaked out? In her innocence she believed that he would be terribly disappointed, even angry, and she could not blame him.

She passed men on foot carrying their packs upon their backs. They were headed for Emigrant Creek. A few minutes later she caught up with a line of wagons and out-of-date contraptions on wheels which had been hurriedly pressed into service.

Emigrant Creek had become the seeming goal of the universe. Most of these people had made similar treks in the past. If this one proved as fruitless as the others they had engaged in they would be just as ready to embark on another. This might be the time. That was the magnet that drew them.

Frazier left them behind, but she saw that others had passed on before her. The marks of automoible tires and shod hoofs were discernible in the deep dust of the road.

It was necessary for her to pass their ranch to get to the creek. It was all she could do to forego turning into the ranch-yard.

Lin had urged her father to go home, and it was with some surprise, therefore, that Frazier heard herself hailed as she rode past the house.

"Lin told me to stop you, Frazier," her father called. "Cantrell got away. McCarroll is on the creek with Kincaid. He fell asleep while he was guarding Cantrell."

Lin would hardly have forgiven himself if he could have seen the effect of this on Frazier.

"There will be a wild time on the creek to-night," Aaron ran on. "I staked a claim. Maybe we'll all get rich after all."

"I'm so glad for Lin's sake," said Frazier. "But he didn't want anyone to know. I passed a small army on my way home. Everyone knows, it seems."

It was well that she didn't go on to the creek. It was cold along the creek. Most of those who came were unprepared for it. Only a few had adequate food and proper utensils for preparing it.

Kincaid and McCarroll were taciturn in the face of what had happened. Surely Cantrell had done his work well.

Men came for a peek at the strike. Lin was deaf to their entreaties. Flash and he sat upon the mine dump with their rifles across their knees.

No one questioned the propriety of this. It is the way of new camps.

The little fires blinking in the darkness along the creek gave no hint of burning out. Claims had been staked all the way down the cañon to Parr's old place. Bits of conversation floated on the air. A stream of profanity greeted them when Lars Svensen's mule knocked down his tent. Somewhere a baby cried.

It was primitive, unlovely, but full of the stuff of life. Kincaid enjoyed it. If his conscience smote him, he kept it to himself.

No wonder Newt Parr tossed in his sleep as he lay beside a purling stream in a lonely cañon far to the west. His troubled spirit must have been back on Emigrant Creek, where he had been the first to drive a drill.

Morning came and brought bedlam. Before noon, Lars Svensen uttered a wild cry that echoed up and down the creek. He had opened a ledge of surface quartz and uncovered a vein of twenty-dollar ore!

Faith in the creek's richness soared. Newcomers arrived to add fuel to the fire.

Kincaid heard the news with such consternation as a man feels but once in a lifetime.

"Svensen's got it?" he demanded incredulously. "Twenty-dollar ore?"

How could he believe it?

He wondered if Cantrell was on the creek. If he had not arrived, he would come soon and hear the latest.

Kincaid smiled. Luck had fallen his way at last.

Shortly after ten o'clock Frazier and her father arrived. Aaron had hired a man to go to town to file his claim for him. He was excited. He went to see Svensen's "find" and from there wandered up and down the cañon listening to all the wild tales one hears in mushroom camps of this sort.

It affected Frazier very differently. She saw that there was nothing good here. The sounds which smote the ear blended into something like the cry of a wolf pack.

They were running together now, but each was waiting and watching for his fellow to fall, ready to rend him limb from limb at the first chance.

Kincaid felt her disgust with what she beheld. He asked her to go home.

"Flash will go with you as far as Parr's place. Did you say anythin' to your father about sellin' out the ranch?"

"Yes, I did. I suppose this excitement had something to do with his answer. He told me he wished he could get rid of the place. But I'm afraid it will come to nothing. Where are we to find a buyer?"

"I'm goin' to supply that very necessary person," Lin said mysteriously. "Either I do that or all this don't make sense," he added, taking in the scene before him with a sweep of his hand. "It was a hundred to one shot when I started playin' it; it ain't that now."

Of course Frazier could not understand him.

"Don't ask me to explain," he hurried to say. "I'm not usually mysterious this way."

He called Flash before saying good-bye to her. Just as she was leaving, she turned to Lin with sudden concern.

"You are not sending me home because you are expecting trouble, are you, Lin?" she asked with great earnestness.

"Why, no!" said he, deeply moved by her thought for him. "There's nothin' to worry about at all."

His thoughts were of her long after she had left. He was brought back to the turbulent present by hearing himself hailed from the creek. It was Spike Dowd and

Chet Dunton, two old Lazy K acquaintances. Their inquiries regarding his whereabouts for the past few weeks may have been inelegant, but they were to the point.

Lin answered with a laugh. He could afford to, he felt. Had he known that they were there on Cantrell's direct order, he would have been doubly pleased. Lin began to suspect as much when he saw Ike Leonard join them. Ike's activities had varied since he retired from the hotel business. Being one of Del's hantly men he was naturally on friendly terms with Cantrell.

The Lazy K men said something to Ike and he turned and waved to Lin.

"Comin' over to see you by-an-by," he called out as though Kincaid and he were the best of friends.

Lin took this friendliness for what it was worth — nothing. But the man's presence held more than passing interest. He knew Ike was close to Cantrell. The very fact that Cantrell had not put in an appearance argued that he had a representative on the creek. It was beyond belief that he could turn his back on this excitement. The logic of this may not be apparent to those unacquainted with Nevada. In that land gold was the master. Cattle meant the daily bread; gold, and gold-hunting, were the romance and adventure of life.

When Ike came up to the tunnel, Lin met him with a smile.

"Went and got yourself a fortune this time, I hear," Ike began. "Ain't nothin' like money to make folks forget the past, boys. That trouble you had over in Elko won't ever be remembered if you take out a million here. I'm glad that's all cleared up over there."

"Who told you it was all settled?" Flash asked.

"Why, I don't know where I heard it," Ike stalled.

"Better admit it was Cantrell," Lin advised.

"It might have been Jim, at that," Ike admitted. "But Lin," he continued, "have you really got it?"

He arrived at his point a little sooner than Kincaid had expected, but Lin was ready for him.

"Take a look," he invited. "I'm satisfied."

"My Lord, man!" Ike exclaimed when he stepped out of the tunnel, "you've got it sure enough. Don't look as if that fault would dip down out of all finding, either. What you agoing to do with it, Lin?"

"Sell it — when the price is right."

Ike concealed his pleasure at this statement.

"Any engineer looked at it yet?"

"Not yet. Blodgett may be up to-day."

And of course he might. Lin did not find it necessary to say that he had not requested him to come.

Ike's conversation drifted to other matters. It was fully five minutes later that he asked what Lin wanted for the mine.

"Oh, I don't know," Lin drawled as though the matter were one he had given no thought. "I guess I'd let her go for twenty thousand. Cash, that is."

Ike shook his head. "You'll never get it. That's too much. You've got to have some ore blocked out before you talk that kind of money."

"Why you so interested?" Lin demanded. "You aren't thinkin' about buyin' me out, are you?"

"Hardly," Ike grinned. "But I've got friends."

"Who? Cantrell?"

"What difference does that make?" Ike queried. "Cantrell's money is just as good as anyone's, whether you like him or not."

"Is he on the creek?"

"No. Won't take me long to get in touch with him if you trim your price down to where it belongs."

Kincaid shook his head.

"That price stands. I've had plenty chances to sell out this mornin'. I'll do business with Cantrell, but at my price, and on one condition."

Ike was hard put to conceal his eagerness. If he knew anything about values, and it was said that he did, this mine was worth a good many times twenty thousand dollars.

"What's the string on it?" he demanded in a tone that implied that the proposition already sounded uninteresting.

"Cantrell's got to buy out the Thanes. I'm not going to waste breath tryin' to tell you why the old man has made such a bust of tryin' to run sheep. If Cantrell wants to do business with me, let him buy out the old man. I'll talk turkey, then."

"That just about kills any chance of my makin' a commission," Ike muttered. "If I *could* put this through, you'd take fifteen for the mine — wouldn't you?"

"If we could close the deal to-day — yes! I may change my mind any minute; that's my privilege."

234

Ike hung on for ten minutes, afraid to let Lin see how anxious he was to be gone.

"He's hooked!" Flash exclaimed when Ike left.

"If Svensen's find doesn't peter out before nightfall — yes. How are we goin' to stand the strain till he comes back?" Lin groaned. "Get a drill, Flash, we'll do a little real minin' this afternoon. It will keep us from goin' mad."

It was good showmanship, too. Lin knew that they were being watched. Visitors were everywhere. Bridger and even the staid Wheeler put in an appearance.

The afternoon wore on as they worked. In the hours they toiled they sunk their drills about three feet. The rock was not particularly hard.

"We quit when this drill gets dull," Flash declared. "I'm bushed, I tell you."

"Suits me," Lin wheezed as he swung the sledge again.

The drill seemed to jump as he hit it. Flash looked up at him with eyes bulging with amazement.

"Hit 'er again, Lin!" he cried.

Lin swung, and their startled eyes saw that the drill had gone in almost to the head.

"We've broke through somethin'," Lin gasped, perspiration dripping from his face.

The madness that he had laughed at in others gripped him now. What had his drill poked its nose into?

He was as nervous as the worst tyro on the creek. His hands actually shook as he removed the drill and prepared to blow out the wall.

McCarroll was no less affected. Speech deserted him.

"Here she goes, Flash!" Lin called as he lit the fuse. "Get a laugh ready; this thing may be just a dream."

Before the smoke had cleared away, Kincaid leaped into the tunnel, straining his eyes to see what the blast had exposed. In that instant he became a stark, raving maniac. They had blown out a pocket of almost pure gold — a yellow honeycomb of precious metal!

There was no estimating its value. It was the sort of "find" that had made millionaires of the Stahl brothers at National.

"Holy suffering Saint Peter and Paul!" Flash cried wildly, "Lady Luck, yore little boy has sure come home! If it's like this here, what must it be way down deep?"

Lin failed to hear him. Reeling, a little sick at thought of how close he had come to handing this fortune to Cantrell for a few thousand dollars, mumbling brokenly to himself, he reached the surface. His fevered cry brought a dozen men to his side. One look, a moment of dreadful silence and then the unleashing of every sound the human voice can utter.

What had passed before was dwarfed to nothing by comparison. Men who had been content to dream of thousands spoke of millions.

Work ceased. Lars Svensen was forgotten. Kincaid's name leaped from lip to lip. He was the hero, the apostle who had led them to the promised land.

A crowd gathered about his mine.

"Tell 'em to go away," Lin muttered to Flash.

Suddenly the crowd parted and Ike Leonard and Cantrell strode forward.

"Here I am," Ike announced. "Jim has bought out old Aaron. Here's your money."

Lin pushed it away and began to shake his head wearily.

"You're too late," they heard him say; "I've changed my mind."

CHAPTER
TWENTY-FIVE

The Long Trail

Cantrell had always been a lone wolf, of course, making use of whoever fell in with his plans. When Ike had come to him with Lin's proposition he had first sworn he would have nothing to do with it. A few words from Ike, and he had changed his mind. Fifteen thousand dollars was about all the cash he could get together; leaving him nothing with which to swing the deal for Aaron's ranch. He did not want the Thane place. Neither did he want to miss a fortune. Accordingly, he cast about for a way to bridge the difficulty.

For two years the Basques had been trying to gain a foothold north of the creek. Here was their chance. Angel was the most likely purchaser.

That this was a deliberate double-crossing of Bridger and the other cattlemen did not weigh at all in Cantrell's deliberations. In fact he found a peculiar satisfaction in getting the best of them behind their backs.

Cagey as usual, he first went to see the old Basque. Nothing but his insatiable greed could have driven him to enter Angel's house, for he knew the man despised him.

238

Angel received him coldly, but with that old-world courtesy which when properly forged is the stoutest armor.

Cantrell's business was quickly stated. Angel expressed his willingness to buy the ranch. Therefore, Cantrell dispatched Ike to find Aaron and bring him to Paradise. By three o'clock the sale had been effected, and Cantrell had taken a profit of a thousand dollars. To be told after all this that Kincaid had changed his mind was more than he could bear.

What might have happened had not Del Ryan pushed his way through the crowd just then, will never be known. That bloodshed could have been averted seems unlikely.

Whatever Del told Cantrell had an immediate effect, for he mounted his horse and disappeared in a cloud of dust.

"He must have seen a ghost," Flash grinned at Lin. "What do you figure Del said?"

Lin could not guess. Before sunset they knew, however. A deputy sheriff from Elko had arrived with a warrant for Cantrell's arrest. He had subpoenas for Lin and Flash, also.

"It's been a great day for the Irish," Flash declared. "Cantrell is on the run; old Aaron has got rid of a lemon; you're rich—"

"And so are you," Lin interrupted.

"What more could you ask?"

"I reckon you know, Flash," Lin murmured as he studied the distant hills.

"I guess I do. Well, she'll be waitin' for you. But Lin, don't ever tell her how this game was worked; she'd never understand or forgive you. No woman would."

Kincaid admitted the wisdom of this.

"With Cantrell loose and this fortune in sight, neither one of us can leave here to-night; but I'll see her in the mornin'. I want to break this news to her myself."

"I'm afraid you won't have that pleasure," Flash remarked. "I reckon there ain't a person but knows already. I hope she won't be tempted to come to the creek to-night. You write her a note. I'll get someone to take it to her."

When the letter was written, Flash went down the creek looking for a messenger to deliver it. He was gone longer than he expected. He was fairly bursting with excitement when he returned.

"My God, Lin," he exclaimed, "Bridger has split with Cantrell over him sellin' the Thane ranch to a Basque. He has charged Cantrell with killing that boy Cèsar. The Basques know and there's hell to pay. Irquieaga is in town steamin' up a crowd to go to the Lazy K and get Cantrell. You know what will happen."

"Don't worry," Lin remarked wisely. "Cantrell will be tipped off in time. I imagine he'll be pretty hard to find come mornin'."

Which was exactly what occurred. As a result Cantrell did not go near the Lazy K that night. He knew it was time for him to leave. Before he went, however, he determined to make one last desperate attempt to get even with Kincaid. If he could not strike

240

at him directly he could hurt him through one who was dearer than life to him.

By morning he had not only planned his attack, but liked it well enough to believe it might succeed. He was ready to try anything, for the matter of that.

By approaching the Thane place in such a way as to keep the barn between himself and the house, he managed to reach the ranch-yard without having been seen by Frazier. She had risen early and was preparing breakfast. Her father still slept.

Cantrell caught a glimpse of her once at the kitchen window. A moment later he knocked at the door.

Frazier opened it at once. In answer to her cry of astonishment and sudden fear at seeing who confronted her, Cantrell leaped through the door and swept her up into his arms.

"You're goin' with me," he snarled as she fought him. "Still a wildcat, eh. You won't scratch much longer."

She was strong, but no match for him. She knocked Cantrell's hand away from her mouth long enough to cry out to her father. By the time Aaron came to the door, Cantrell was in his saddle with Frazier in his arms.

Aaron had lately purchased a rifle. When he had located it, Cantrell was half a mile away and heading for the Reserve. Even as he ran to the barn to saddle his horse Aaron knew that neither he nor his mount were any match for Cantrell and his fleet-footed sorrel. And yet, he could only follow, hoping against hope that some miracle would deliver Cantrell to him. Help was far away. He thought of Lin and Flash. Cantrell would be in Idaho before they could be told.

He was about to leave when a party of horsemen, riding at full gallop, swooped towards the house. He did not have to look twice to know that they were Basques. They did not sit in their saddles the way Westerners do. Their style of riding had been borrowed from the moor. Irquieaga, who was an excellent horseman, wheeled his foam-covered mount with a flourish and brought the animal up all trembling.

"Cantrell here?" he demanded. "We look for heem all night."

"There he goes!" Aaron cried, pointing to the hills. "He's kidnapped my daughter. Stop him, Irquieaga! Stop him!"

They dashed away as wildly as they had come. Ten minutes later they almost ran down Kincaid, on his way to see Frazier and very well satisfied with the world this morning. It did not take long to acquaint him with what happened. When they reached the Reserve, Lin turned to the north, certain that Cantrell's objective was Idaho.

It was a slashing ride, even for him, He knew this country as well as Cantrell. When Kincaid finally picked up the other's trail he was dumbfounded to see that it held to the east. Didn't Cantrell know that he had an impassable gorge ahead of him?

Cantrell knew what he was doing. The rangers had built a footbridge across the cañon. Once across he attacked the bridge with the axe he had found in Aaron's barn. He had bound Frazier hand and foot when she threatened to leap into the creek, boiling below.

There was some timber along the cañon at this point. Therefore, Kincaid was within three hundred yards of the bridge before Cantrell saw him. Lin dashed forward. Big Jim swung his axe more lustily than ever. Suddenly the bridge sagged. The sound of splintering timbers filled the air. Another blow and the bridge plunged down into the abyss.

Kincaid was armed, but before he could get within revolver range, Cantrell sped away. When he judged himself safe he pulled up his horse and stopped to see what Kincaid would do now.

"Am I licked?" Lin groaned. "If I only had a rifle!"

He thought of his good fortune of yesterday. What did it mean now? Riches without her meant little. An old poplar, dead and bare, stood upon the opposite brink. Lin knew he could get his rope over it and swing himself across, but this chase had only begun. He had to have Piñon to win it.

Willing though he was to take any desperate chance with death to get across, he could not ask Piñon to try to leap the gorge. No, not here, but there was a place to the north where the cañon narrowed! But Cantrell would be a mile away by that time.

Lin remembered the Basques, then. They were circling around to the east far below. If Cantrell tarried much longer he must find them in his way. With that thought to buoy him up, Kincaid turned Piñon to the north and galloped off. Cantrell's cruel laughter floated down to him. Turning in his saddle, Lin saw Big Jim lope away.

The spot where Lin hoped to cross seemed wider than he had believed. All of the momentum of Piñon's great speed would be necessary to carry the animal over. To fail meant death for both.

He let the horse see what he had to do. Backing away then for a hundred yards, he tensed himself for the charge.

"I wouldn't ask this of you for myself, old-timer," he muttered, as he stroked Piñon's glossy coat. "It'll take your best to make it."

It was literally a leap for life. Lin rose in his stirrups as Piñon sailed into space. He had a flash of the creek running white over the rocks far below.

He felt the horse sinking. The momentum of that furious charge was almost gone. Did enough remain to carry them across?

Even as he wondered, Piñon struck the opposite bank and rolled over, throwing Lin free and knocking the wind completely out of him.

Minutes passed before he sat up. Piñon was eyeing him curiously. Lin limped over to him and felt his legs.

"You all right, old-timer?" he exclaimed tenderly. "What a horse you are!"

They began to leave the creek behind, then. Far ahead of them, Cantrell had become aware of the Basques blocking his way. He turned back. Before long he saw Kincaid in full cry after him. Fire was his only salvation now. He did not hesitate to resort to it.

Lin had not caught sight of Cantrell, but the clouds of smoke which began to rise drew his attention and then he saw the big fellow riding with it as a screen between them.

"He'll trap himself now!" Lin muttered savagely. "Wait until this wind really gets behind it!"

Cantrell soon realized the truth of this. Faster than his horse could run the flames swept around the mountain, burned upward, with Cantrell falling back before the steadily advancing line of fire.

"They'll be burned to death," Kincaid groaned. "Where is Remmington with his plane? He might get them out!"

All thought of pursuit was gone now. To find the ranger was his only thought. Remmington had been apprised of the fire. He was ready to take to the air when Kincaid dashed up and flung himself from Piñon's back.

"Cantrell and Miss Thane are on that mountain," he shouted. "Let me climb in with you. If you can fly low enough, maybe I can get a rope to 'em!"

"I can't land there," the ranger shouted back. "If I can see, I'll skim the grass for you."

"There they are!" Lin yelled in the ranger's ear as they circled lower and lower over the flaming mountain. "That bare spot to the right!"

Remmington nodded and sent the plane lower and lower.

Kincaid climbed out upon the wing of the plane. Bracing himself, he shouted to Cantrell. Both Frazier and big Jim were staring up at him. Cantrell had unbound her. They understood what he was trying to do.

Several times Kincaid's long noose just missed Frazier. The smoke was getting thicker, the fire coming nearer.

"Better make it this time," Remmington warned.

Lin tried again and almost lost his balance as Frazier was drawn into the air. She was unconscious when Lin dragged her into the plane. They came back for Cantrell, then.

"I can't see," the ranger called. "Where is he?"

Lin pointed out the spot where Cantrell had stood. He threw his rope, but it came up empty.

"I'm afraid he's gone," Remmington said.

"Try once more; last time!"

Cantrell was not to be seen.

"The smoke got him," Lin shouted.

Remmington soared high now.

"My men will have a job putting this out," he said to Kincaid. "I can't take you home."

Soon after they had returned to the ranger's cabin, Frazier was able to sit up. Lin told her that Cantrell was dead.

"God forgive him," she whispered.

When he thought her able to start for home he pointed to Piñon.

"He's waitin' for us," he murmured. "He's carried us both before, as I reminded you once."

Frazier had been told what the horse had done.

"You're as brave as your master, Piñon," she whispered in his ear.

"My horse can't have any secrets from me," Lin smiled. "What are you telling him?"

"You'll have to guess, Lin," she blushed.

It was a ride never to be forgotten by either.

"I suppose you will blossom out with a great ranch, now," Frazier mused.

"No," Lin said decisively. "Everybody tries to rip out a fortune in this state. Nevada hasn't a thing to show for the money men have taken out of her. Some day that'll be changed. No one has taken away the creeks. That water is goin' to mean farms in the end. I'm goin' to set by myself for that day."

Frazier gazed at him proudly.

"I think I'd like to be included in that dream, Lin," she said ever so softly.

"I reckon you've always been included. I told you long ago that you'd marry me some day."

"I hope you'll not keep me waitin' long," she sighed as he bent and kissed her.

"I was thinkin' about to-morrow."

"To-morrow?" she gasped.

"Well, maybe we could make it to-day," he teased.

"No, to-morrow will do, dear."